ENTANGLED SOULS

P. S. Gusain

Invincible Publishers

First Printing: 2019

ISBN: 978-81-943134-8-9

Invincible Publishers

Registered Address: 201A, SAS Tower, Sector 38, Gurugram - 122003

DEDICATION

TO

LOVE

ENTANGLED SOULS

MY WIFE AND DAUGHTER

ACKNOWLEDGEMENT

I take this opportunity to acknowledge the love and care of my family, friends, and others whom I might not have reciprocated fairly and adequately.

In fact, Entangled Souls is my acknowledgement of their love and the sincere attempt to express, howsoever insufficiently, my love.

I take this opportunity to also thank all of them, including Invincible Publishers, for their kindness and support.

When I look back in melancholy, I find only a vast ocean of regrets of not loving to my heart's content and not thanking enough those who loved and cared for me.

Our parents die before we could dissuade ourselves from the notion that they would live forever and there would be enough time later to love and serve them!

In the rat race for more and more, we have less and less time to love our children and spouse and others.

To acknowledge the ersatz applause of the captive audience, we let the hand of our soulmate slip by from our grip and blinded by the limelight of fame and fortune do not see love's silent retreat to backstage and out of our life!

When we untangle the Entangled Souls, they stealthily disappear from our life leaving a void in our hearts which can never be filled.

Love is NOW or NEVER!

Oh! The heartache of missing on loving.

(P. S. Gusain)

CONTENTS

Pining

'Tis better to have loved and lost
Than never to have lost at all'
'Tis better to have loved and lost
Than never to have loved at all'

The best that could happen to anybody
Is falling in love with somebody
Still better, yet, is being loved
Bliss when both fall in love together

Many things must happen, do happen often
Before a lad becomes a man, a lass, a woman
One has not grown really till one has loved
How does it matter, whether won or lost?

I loved you, but denied to myself
Thought life is greater, goes beyond love
Oh! Life is perdition without you, My Love!
I understood it too late, too desperate!

What else is there in life after loving you?
Loving you on the heath under the rains
Loving you on the golden beach awash in moon
Loving you half-buried in the snowflakes!

Simply being together, you around the household
Talking, laughing, walking hand in hand
Even afar knowing you love me, I love you
Dearest! My life is defined in terms of you!

All the happiness in the world comes my way
What's it without sharing it with you

Tiny thorn pricks me, ever so little pain
Saddest thought, with you a rose were in hand!

Oh! Dear, the thought of you away from me!
Tears, maladies, mishaps, myriad of ill omens
Who caresses lullabies, kisses sleep away in the morn
Oh! Who pampers, cajoles, spoils, and makes you laugh?

I think of you every moment, all times
You'd have said this, done that
You'd have smiled then, cried now
My life something else when we together

You are too much with me
A joy, your thought invoked, heartache
Farewell joy, harbinger of sweet pain
Sadness, now you are my joy

How sweet is this sadness you gave me
I would not barter it for happiness
Addicted to this sour-sweet pain
I know, I shall never be happy again

The valley is full of deep, dense fog
Below, the river of life flows still
Gone to bottom are the fish of joy
No birds sing here, no breeze blows

The table is still laid for two
First spoonful, bite, sip is offered to you
We still sleep entwined, I dare not stir
Lest, far away, your sweet dream be broken!

The rose blossoms, falls, lost, forgotten
Tear-soaked letters, album, withered flowers
We still live, eat, and sleep together
Only you don't smile and I miss your kiss

You still help me with my tie, buttons
I invoke you thousands of times in a day
Unawares, I talk to you in my loneliness
We smile, laugh, then weep, together

You live with me in all things small and big
I leave space for your name at each stanza
And your love name sacred and sweet
Is now my password for all things!

Let me whisper goodnight on your lips
When you go to sleep, too contented and relaxed
Like a baby who has sucked to the fill
Till the firm breasts of the mother limp

Let me tickle you on the navel
And make you laugh, till tears flow
'We laugh too much, we shall weep'
I weep too much, shall I ever laugh?

When the sky is blue and fields gilded green
Butterfly leaves waltz on the music of Zephyr
She glides down on the golden wings of radiance
Hovers over copses and sprawls across meadows
Tender morn breeze lifts her misty, silky veil
She turns her radiant face to me and smiles
My heart misses a beat, it runs amuck
It leaps up and flies into her lap!

She is far away like a sheet of sunbeams
Of the daystar behind clouds betwixt mountains
Then she runs to me limbs flailing, vestments flying
Now covering now uncovering her beauteous body

Oak foliage swaying in the monsoon like whirling Dervish
Her verdant drape flips up marble white breasts
The flimsy wrap flies away, lo! It's a vagabond cloud
Sunray caressed you, in ecstasy became rainbow!
Disrobed, she runs riding violent storms
Her body drenched and hair dishevelled
And knocks at my heart, it opens
We are splashed with all the red of desire
We glide through rains, rivulets, meadows, woods
Through mist and fog, heath and thicket
And make leaf boats to sail on them
To the land of dreams and love!

She is all white, shower of lily petals
Cold lips on my cheeks, nose, ears, and bites
Oh! Madness, flame of desire, embrace
So firm, she melts away in my arms

We make an igloo, and shut the world out
Snow, snow everywhere, it snows all night
It falls ever so softly like my tender kisses
When you murmur my name in sweet dreams

The sky is azure, air as clear as your eyes
Glimmering leaves dance in the arms of the breeze
You in tartan skirt with basketful of flowers
Stumbling embrace, cascading flowers, silken laughs
The stimulant ambrosial breeze is also soporific

Birds sound reveille on a lullaby air
Cocooned in snug embrace, spell of entwined limbs
You want to return home, yet want not to

Fairest *Menaka*[1] gathers her lingerie from empyrean bed
Made of purest white vapours, soft and translucent
And wraps herself up in star-studded gown
Oh! The cold, emptiness, crushed roses and lilies

When I see around the vast expanse of my life
Rippling sea under the sinking sun, gentle breeze
I look back to the wake of the sparkling foam
Ahead the swath of twinkling light of gentle sun

It's you, dear! Around, behind, beyond
The foamy expanse, glimmering Milky Way
It's dark and lonely, a wandering ship
An albatross around the neck, accurst me

A red red kiss on still redder heart
Blossoms into a flaming rose, roseate fire
When the embrace is broken, beloved gone
What remains—a cosy pain, an aching joy

I'm a wounded fledgeling, shivering in the rains
Whose flock has migrated to distant lands
I'm the lost sheep in the dense woods
Whose shepherd has returned home to sleep

If I kiss another girl and think of you
I'd vitiate the trusting proffered lips
If I kiss another girl and not think of you
The saddest-happiest day, pallbearers and *Kahars*[2]

If I love again I would spoil her
I'd love her better than I did you
I loved you badly, I'm wiser now
Oh! How much I'd love my second love!

I drink to forget you, forget all else
I remember you all the more drunk
My body craves for you, my heart, my soul
Oh! How much I desire you when drunk!

Your memory comes like a wisp of cloud
Solitary streaking through serene sunny sky
Where from, where to, who knows?
Oh! The void in the sky of my heart
Sky is serene, we two together, quiet and happy
A stray cloud hurrying to amorous rendezvous
Your thought, a whiff of fragrance in my heart
Floats and spreads and permeates all
Sometimes it gathers like a speck on the horizon
Spreads and multiplies to darken the boundless sky
My heart sheds torrents of tears all night
The body is still inflamed like a funeral pyre

My Penelope, keep on weaving and undoing the robe
Let the wooden horse be made, the war over
No Calypso, no Circe, can bewitch me for keeps
I'll return to you as the sun to the sea
To slay brutally and painfully the train of suitors
Fairweather friends, underlings cringed before me
Crowding my sky in shiny robes pestering my moon
All because I'm not there to fade them away!

I'm condemned to death, yet have the cell key
Outside I see sunshine, smiles and free life
Take away your key! Bewitch me not!
This cell is reality, out there mirage and illusion

Let the world be as beautiful as ever
There are other lovers, let them enjoy
Let me burn in the fire of your love
I'll be consumed, or shine as gold

Dear rains do not tap at windowpanes
Kind snow, why cool heels in the courtyard?
Friendly sun enter not through slits and sills
Why torture me? Leave me alone, let me die!

Your embrace is all the riches for me
Power to love you and retain your love
Fame enough to be known as true lover
How less a man needs, how much desires?

The festival of colours is here, spring in flowers
It's time for lights and crackers and sweets
Every soul is drenched in colours, every eye radiant
Why then my heart is dry, soul in utter dark
I'm also under the shower of colours
I've also lighted a few earthern lamps
Merry Xmas! Drunk I too shout with others
Why then, Oh! Why, happiness is shy of me?
Am I lotus-leaf which water wets not
A hard brittle mirror, reflects but absorbs not
Is happiness a drop of mercury?
On the palm, but impossible to grab!

Saints aim for *Moksh*[3], eternal bliss
Reunion with God, freedom from desires
And the cycle of birth and death
Sinner me! I prefer your love to all!

People take with them their deeds–good or bad
I'll take with me only your memories
And won't care He puts me in Hades or Elysium
Wherever you are it's heaven, hell where not

In the morn when you are still deep asleep
I sit beside you and put my trembling fingers
In your tresses, on your lips and breasts
A kiss on the forehead, a tip-toe embrace
Alas! The magic touch is gone, stir you not
No arms encircle me and pull into the folds
Even when I make to move, you do not protest
And pull me back or call me in whispered shouts

A thin sheet of sliced moment separates us
A breath of air, a missed beat of heart
My bare feet crunch the morning frost and bleed
Oh! You lying lifeless in polka-dotted red

Oh! Dual drops of tears in your limpid eyes
Milk oozing forth from small firm breasts
Unconscious mother, stillborn sweet child
Dark misty night, a pair of binary stars

Small trickles on cheeks, *Ganga-Jamuna*[4] at source
A beaded pearl necklace, unstrung at breasts
Shooting stars, dew droplets on red rosebuds
Molten lava dripping down my frozen heart

The body of a girl is softer than
The evanescent kiss—tears and adieu
That moment is weak and sacred, so she
Touch her, Oh! Only with the tenderest kisses

Her heart is fragile, you in my dawn dream
Shattered to myriad smithers, irrevocable loss
Keep it cocooned in love, deepest recess of heart
Greatest sin is breaking heart of Eve, bravo Adam!

Our love story is written on the blue sky
In God's hand, His own letters, eternal and bright
The great Muralist painted the dome long ago
Yet each motion, each emotion of it He foresaw
We in tight embrace or you alone with a mirror
We sitting together, talking all night
Or, I till morn abiding you at the door
Each moment pulsates with its own life
It's better than life where each coming moment
Erases or alters the present, numbs the emotions
Permanency, even the state of being, an illusion
Sweet pain of waiting is spoiled by the reunion
The magic of the moment is vibrant in the stars
In the space of an instant is *freezed* the timeless
Here the embrace is eternal so the separation
Runs though fast, the Leo shall never catch the Aries

My star beamed bright and full in the sky
Till it began to play hide and seek with me
You are still there, only I peer not hard
Oh! The void in the sky of my heart
Cruel far-darter! Broken dream, embrace, heart
Who cares for thy tinsel trinkets of golden hue?

Thou killed my star that shone steadfast
With a single ray of light which pierced the sky
In vain they shine, sun, moon and countless stars
When mine is lost which shone for me alone
Was it already lost when its rays first reached me?
Love was then foredoomed, why I still hope?

I wander among the stars, they wink at me
Ah! The flesh is weak and the heart is lonely
But my body goes numb, my heart sinks
Oh! Pity me, I cannot gaze at another star!
Now and then some star looks like you
But the illusion is shattered 'ere I look twice
Shut the window, draw the curtains, close my eyes
You are gone, wipe out the stars!
When I die let not my eyes be closed
Bury me on a snowy knoll close to stars
Let me gaze eternally upon the void in starry sky
And lament and weep over the double loss

The bride is all ready to depart yet lingers on
Amongst her wardrobe, letters and albums of a lass
Pranks, frolics, tears and smiles, bosom friends
Crowd around her and nudge her forward yet pull in
Forget! Burn!! Banish all!!! Letters, albums, memoirs
Wipe off tears forever, never utter my name again
Burn the past to ashes, Phoenix-like conjure it not
When they talk of love, smile but seal the lips
Step out in all bridal finery to the handsome groom
Ride the limousine bedecked in flowers, balloons, festoons
Amidst cavalcade of smiles, laughs, videos and honking
To the bridal bed covered with blood-red burning roses
New joys, new smiles, new laughs, God bless you

In love and care, you build your new homestead
Let there be a little girlie in the image of yourself
Then stealthily slip out of girlhood and be a woman
God bless you the happiness we dreamt together
What will I do with my share all-alone!
Yet hide just two droplets of tears in the heart
To furtively shed when you hear I cease to be

Hell is to wish time past to come back
To wish undone or redone, done and sealed
To turn and toss on the rack all night
To lie bleeding pierced by the spear of *If*

It's heaven to have won love
And lost everything else forever
It's hell to have lost love
For everything else in life!

I loved you but forgot to own you
And cared little for time and space
I had you in my arms, I was content
I loved you too much, so I lost you, Dearest!

NOTES

1=One of the most beautiful celestial nymphs who was sent by Indr, king of gods, to lure *Vishwamitr* away from his *tapasya* (austerities) in which she succeeded.
2=Bearers of palanquin of a bride.
3=Liberation (from the cycle of birth and death), Oneness with God.
4=Two of the most important rivers of North India.

Meeting

The souls wander in the wilderness
Their journey has no beginning, middle, or end
Source not the takeoff, sea not the goal
Eternity to eternity, lives lived to rebirths

My love is a spark out of divine love
It's Universal Love, that of all lovers
Lovers gone by, present, to come
I is not me, you not merely my beloved

Love is infinite, eternal, without beginning and end
The cause of Creation, Preservation, and Destruction
Beyond categories, qualities, limitations, *Neti...Neti*[1]
Love is always love, God unkind and cruel sometimes!

God saw into the void and felt lonely, utterly lonely
That first emotion was so strong, even today
Amidst the universe of humanity, we find us lonely
The first surge of energy, still moves the stars

He created mind-born sons, like Himself
In meditation, they neglected procreation
In anger, He produced *Rudr*[2], half-male, half-female
Manu Svayambhuv[3], divided into male and female

He divided One into two for procreation
But two need to be one for the same
Sex is the urge to be one again
Where's sin or shame in it?

Then came Creation, and *Yugs*[4], even other Gods
Wars won and lost, deluges, droughts, famines

Great nations rose and fell, kings and queens
Sex and love saved man, mind shall annihilate

We met as might meet two wandering stars
On identical co-ordinates in space-time
Are we One separated like earth and moon forever?
But bound by some invisible force till eternity

Was it a mere chance I met you
Like two old friends in a crowded bazaar
Happy spin of a coin, a pseudo-random machine
Fate working unnoticed in the garb of chance

I was born to fly like an eagle
Above the earth, beyond clouds, into the stars
Even beyond in the land of dreams and fantasies
Where light bends, space curves, time topsy-turvy

When I was born, running was in vogue
Man had already flown high and swam deep
Running was different, the feel of something solid
Smooth well-trodden paths, clearly visible goals

I ran, hopped, tried hard, all seemed well
Till on difficult terrain, I stumbled and fell
The abyss of ignominy and mire, bruised and stunned
Rendering overjoyed the so-called near and dear ones

How could a flier of skies stumble and fall
Here I was down and out, valley of dejection
Oh! The shame, impotent rage, desire to die
Nightmare, surreal things happening in unreal world

Some failures we cause, others fall from the sky
Some lurk in the dark, waiting to ambush us
Some are friendly shake-ups, others rude shocks
Some are like poison which vitiate whole life

Oh! The escape into the heart's dark cosy den
Licking of the wounds all alone, tears and pain
Pestering flies, gleeful jackals awaiting the end
Desire to slumber and sleep, the sleep of death
Wish to be invisible or be erased like a blot
To duck known faces like debtors and shamed
To run away from home, friends and the world
And roam and wander like a nomad or vagabond
Ah! The self-pity, blame on fate and chance
The world of fantasy, daydream and dejection
The eternal regret, 'I could have been...if...'
The anguished cry for 'one, only one, more chance'

In the morn the judgment is to be read
I know it shall be 'To be hanged till death'
Hope, immortal hope, the great solace and sustain
In the darkest of nights, my hope shines brightest!

Who knows tomorrow the world itself may end
What a perverted hope, I call death even faster!
Or, the court deluged, judge writes all wrong
He whom I killed might walk right into the court!

Next day the sun rose as is its wont
The court sat as usual, judge sane as ever
No dead man ever walked into the court
Verdict–'Guilty. To be Hanged till Death!'

I lament and re-lament and lament again and again
Again and again lament and re-lament and lament I
The needle screeches in the concentric grooves
It sticks fast at the crack and gnaws at the heart
I see life in still or motion–normal, slow or fast
Sometimes forward and sometimes in reverse
In colour or black and white, even upside down
I reduce or enlarge it, see close-up or wide-angle
Ah! The self-delusion of a condemned man
Hope against hope for the miracle, for the Saviour
All through night, the final bath, the black mask
The ultimate solace, life after death, immortal soul

Smug and snug in mire, soothing balm on heart sores
Indolent hemlock, numbing pain, lullaby of death
Strange pride and masochism in being martyr of fate
Forget all dreams, live in death, and be content

I lay in the deep pit, Icarus like
So dark I could see stars in the sky
Mosquitoes, gnats and flies, far above crows
Buzzed and croaked, as if lords of the sky

They were not even flying, resting on their oars
Friendly wind, impetus of the opportune jump
Keeping them afloat and taking to greater heights
Late out of the starting block, abandon or run on

Yet life is not a sprint, rather a marathon
Here even slow and steady may win the race
Maybe trudging and persevering I scale heights
To which no mortal can ever reach even flying

Life is a mad rush for a few vehicles
Some know what to grab, others undecided
A few positioned well to reach, others not so lucky
Some fight not, fools queue, some value tradition

They get what they could reach to in a medley
Of qualifications, efforts, luck, fouls, accidents
Cars, buses, motorcycles, cycles and on foot
This motley caravan is now on the road

Bar accidents, inhuman feats, all is settled for life!
Vehicles give comfort and shelter only, not happiness
It comes from rain and sunshine, helping others along
Destination end of road, not goal, goal is the road

Can a lion be better pet than a dog?
A king a better courtier, bend more to kowtow
Oh! The inadequacy of great men in mean positions
Rivals that of fools with power, fame and fortune
Often I realize, it was better I had fallen
I know now success and happiness are not one
How beautiful the earth is, how loveable man
Now I fly surveying the earth not the stars

If I were not me, the fall was the end
I seemed to reconcile but tried hard to fly
Like the proverbial frog churned and churned
Till the milk became butter and it jumped out

They applauded, some real happy, others shammed
Yet I felt cheated and ashamed of myself
The victory reminded me only of the defeat
Best years of life lost, I lagged far behind

I came to you with this wound at heart
Returned with another, deeper and fatal
Same heartache and anguish, life *déjà vu*
Survive I again, this time the will is missing
I had come out of the dreary death pit
I worked hard to recover the lost time
Won a research grant in your country
In the National University of your land

Fledged again, I flew, my heart soared skyward
Above trees, houses, slums, criss-cross roads
Above and beyond the saline fields, the shoreline
Higher till foam and sailboats merged, disappeared

Farewell, dear ones; farewell, rejoicers of my fall
I leave my joys and sorrows all behind
I leave my country, my land, go beyond oceans
To live a new life, till I come back

The downy bed of clouds, so dense and inviting
I could jump into them and float till eternity
A voyage in the rainbow boat where with bolts
Krishn[5] bursts the brim-full pitchers of the *Gopis*[6]

I flew still higher into the vault of heaven
And knew not I was nearer the sea or sky
Like in a trance, I forgot time and space
And kept hearing the primordial Om[7]

Moon came and brought with her countless stars
As your thought comes with myriad of memories
Arrogant man! Rivals thou God with tiny lamps
Oh! Where will you find, the only, my lost moon?

Out of the sea rose together in east and west
The fiery ball of light and the great continent
Left or right, above or below, imbibe I what
How much I wish I were not one but two!

Oh! The inadequacy of one body in loving well
How can lonely me fulfil your body, your heart
Only one body, one heart, your mad abandonment
Insane frenzy of lust, greed, and bestowal

The Fire and Deluge consume each other, all calm
A ship gone berserk in raging violent sea
Two fires meet and embrace with countless limbs
Mad, mad, mad, together we made each other mad

How vaporous and mirage-like is the dividing line
One penetrates deep, other mad waves, whirlpools
We see only the surface, down under both are same
Love and sex and love, I and you and I

I wandered and lingered on, my heart aquiver
Rosebud in bridal red on moonlit foliage bed
An innocent lovely schoolgirl at the window seat
Hesitating to drop 'I love you' into eager hands

I turned and flew low over the great continent
You half asleep beside me in the matin hours
Grey as departing night, fresh as morning breeze
In dawn desires, memories of night pleasures

Twin hillocks firm and erect, deep gorge half-hidden
Vast vale, red canyon, swift overpowering currents

Plateau land to lie down gazing into stars, and talk
Deep, dark, dense forests, wanderlust of whole life

Sudden plunge, you push up to meet halfway
Grinding treads, rushing breaths, pressed wings
Oh! I come, a stranger, would become the Dearest
Alas! I would leave soon, life, miserable life!

Waking up from sound sleep in the morn
One knows not what first saw and heard, felt
The empty bed, sounds in the kitchen, aroma of tea
Chirping birds, hustle-bustle outside, mingled in one

At first senses are confused, they get focused
One sees, comprehension dawns, emotions arise
First big things, hills, forests, rivers, houses
Then only come faces, smiles, tears and laughs

Many things happened to me together, some later
Some understood and felt at once, others slowly
I do telescope and kaleidoscope time and events
Time may flow in reverse and light often zigzag

Like lightning strikes the heart beauty of Eve
Yet it's the shower of tender words and smiles
Which captivates the heart like the army on foot
After the fortress has been pounded by the guns

Nubile lass attires herself some days in primrose
Rambles through meadows flashing tinsel sunny smile
Tall grass in autumnal tints tousling golden tresses
Her gossamer misty garb ruffles, unfurls and flies
She runs for it, moon after a silvery haze for cover

Bump! Oh! She bumps into my vagabond lonely heart
Stunned, stands still in her pristine naked beauty
Covers with hands her body, her face, then mine eyes
In turn she reveals more than what she hides
And her touch breaks the spell of abundant beauty
Sightless I grope, we embrace and kiss on the lips
Infinite beauty, eternal embrace, immortal kiss!
Misty garb lost, revealed, shy maiden is all abandon
Supine lies along the boulevard carefree sunbathing
Oh! The virgin beauty, soft curvaceous fragrant body
How much is spoiled and lost in the garb of modernity

Dear! Let my lips trace the contours of your body
Like a monarch a map 'this much is mine'
Let me live and die within these bounds
All the rest is mirage, unreality, hearsay!

Did I really see, embrace and kiss her
Me a mortal, she vaporous spirit and divine
Was it a revelation, God gives to prophets, devotees?
Why me, why here, why on the very first day

Revelation comes to those who are ripe for it
It comes in odd places, at unexpected times
Faithfuls understand it, accept without questioning
Doubting Thomases distrust and ponder, then accept

It came to Muhammad in the cave at Mount Hira
To *Nanak Dev*[8] in the river *Baeen*[9], Buddh under fig tree
Moses had it at Mount Horeb, Hindus on *Himalayas*
Vohu Manah led Zoroaster, Holy Spirit revealed to Christ

I would stand and stare for hours at a brook
Sprawl on grass on a meadow under the rains
Walk on the snow when it is falling still more
Overjoyed by a beam of moon or a twinkling star
Nature gave me frenzied ecstasy of religion
It over-powered my soul and my heart
I knew all its varying moods and shades
I laughed and talked with her for hours

It was a typical rainy December day
My colleague was telling me about the passing sights
Names of buildings, bridges, roads, landmarks
Then we were in the downtown of high risers

We passed through National Park Causeway
To the Pearly Gate bridge astride Burrow inlet
Then up the winding roads of West City
To a beautiful house, my house, on Crescent Drive

I went up and gasped, oh, what a beauty, what a view!
The entire downtown lay in front of me
Directly was the Pearly Gate bridge, high above waters
Joining North Shore to the City through National Park

The city looked like an architectural model on a platter
The sails of Sailors Den looked like a ship anchored
Beyond lay The Archipelago of unending forest beaches
This side of water, on my left, was North City

I had heard much about your beautiful city
The Land of Liquid Sunshine, sea and mountains
Fame often pampers hope, leading her to despair
What a joy when beauty over-reaches renown

Oh! The joys of solitude, the bliss of a recluse
Lying under a cool bower beside a humming stream
Like a drowsy child in the lap of a fairy
Still night in the embrace of a book of romance

A single star in the clear sky serene in solitude
A lark soaring high heavenwards happy and content
A solitary stream dancing down slippery rock floor
A lonely nightingale crooning a solo joyous song

Sea is calm, waves scoops of sunshine
Sky is blue, the air warm and still
A skiff drifts lazily, my senses drowsy
In my bosom lies the heart snug and cosy

The joy in my heart does not burst out
As does the beauty and joy of a bud
It lies cocooned in the palm of the pain
In chrysalis sweet sorrow as saline joy

All was not God and Creation and reading
There were comic moments of single life too
If man is the King of his castle, why is he
So clumsy in his kingdom without a Queen!

First the kitchen, sanctum sanctorum of women
Resents the presence of man in various ways
A man stands for hours near the milk pot
The moment he turns his back, it spills over!
The soup burns, then the pot, lo and behold!
There is a gaping hole in the casserole!
The man, unawares, is immersed in a novel
Musing, how easy it is to cook food!

On a rainy day, confident, I thought of *Samosas*[10]
Put oil on the fire day-dreaming culinary honours
Only to find myself engulfed in dark smokes
All the rooms had to be repainted thrice!
Anything can happen to a man in the kitchen
He may become a modern artist making breads[11]
Fatalist when rice is uncooked or soggy
Stoic in salt and chillies, narcissist in all

The world lets not a lonely man alone
Phone and doorbell ring at odd hours
When he is in the toilet or taking a bath
Taking his meal or trying to doze off
Modern man is Pavlov's dog, conditioned
It rings he can't remain still
Only to find a wrong number, a promo call
A salesman, somebody who is not welcome

To sleep hungry, too lazy to come down
To slump on sofa too drunk to climb up
Nostalgic melancholy descending like dusk
Benumbing of senses, blithesome oblivion

There was a void, a suspense, in my heart
Not lust of the body, I knew it not then
Not need for the company to while away time
I could live in a jungle for years, all alone

It was akin to the desire of the lonely God
To be two, create, and give meaning to Himself
God without qualities is formless nothing
Life without love is abyss, meaningless nothing

My soul desired you, my heart throbbed for you
The flesh craves a caress, a kiss, an embrace
On the odyssey of love, the soul, heart and body
Met unawares like two ships on their separate ways

Dreamlike let me reach there in advance of time
As reaches a pilgrim the temple of the Goddess
And be with you before I wake and restart
The never-ending journey to your shrine, alone

To recall a seed from a tree is possible
The pencil sketch from the enigmatic Mona Lisa
But not what you looked like that first day
From the face which is now engraved on my soul
On that face are super-imposed all our days together
Love, sex, smiles, tears, hope and despair, many more
Showers, snow, spring, sun, sand, sea, and sky
Short days, shorter nights, *bientфt matins, bienvenue soirťes*
Birthdays, Xmases, New Years, once a year days
Parties, outings, clubs, drinks, dance and Julio
Dominoes or rummy, quiet evenings or nights in embrace
A whole new face when we two alone

A memory comes with a whole set of sensations
Which makes the thing remembered something new
Your face is not only a face it's my kisses too
In your face reflected I see my love
Your face as it comes to me today
Is the carving of years of tender love
Which each caress, each day gave new shape
Yet the sculptor had seen it all the first day
I've eidetic imagery of you, better than photographs
It's exact yet alive and ever-changing with time

Susceptible to subtle suggestions, quirk of fancy
Oh! Sometimes you even come alive, we talk and love!

Oh! The face in the glow of naked body
Body, mind and soul too make and change a face!
That face is free from all daytime cares
Feelings, emotions, smiles, routine expressions
Even sunshine gives the face a false look
And the fact of being seen makes it unnatural
How to put in words how that face looks like
One can say it may look like a face in sleep
No, in sleep eyes are closed and body unconscious
It's a face in pure bliss or complete submission

You look beautiful in all moods, all times
But the most beautiful face I would nobody saw
All bliss in the mellow glow of lambent love
Seen in the bed from very near from just above!

So do perhaps I mix what I saw later
With the impression of the day first far away
On that first day, I might not have remarked
Except a face very much to my heart

Poets have praised for aeons the face of Eve
The full moon, a pink rose in early bloom
A lily of purest white bathed in morning dew
Made of fairest things, marble, snow and cream

Her face is the radiant dome of the sky
Above mountain range in silhouette on the horizon
In hazy veil of wandering vapours light and misty
When the sun is rising, moon and stars not left yet

Sun in its shining raiment is still indoors
And the sky is clear and calm and serene
I clearly discern the rising raiment of light
Sky and sea bathed in the sheen of luminosity

Beautiful as the undulating hills and mounds of sand
In the falling dusk when there is little light below
Seen from above floating on clouds at the centre of
Celestial dome pink at the rim, smile on your face

I sit for hours musing beside the soft-flowing river
Resplendent in gold, smiling in pink roses, all beautiful
Then she bares her body, golden limbs embrace me
All's light and soft around me, Ah! The supreme beauty

Light disguises things in the veil of colour and hue
Poetry in paraphrase, a portrait under mega glass
Gone! The pristine shape and form, daylight murder
Ah! Under the pall of light lies moon pallid and dead

A face is pinpricks and stubble under microscope
And the telescope dots moon face with pockmarks
How ugly light makes things adding senseless details
Beatific beauty, light disintegrates it into cluster of dots
I wake up at midnight as if called by love name
And somnambulist-like follow you up the rooftop
Lo and behold! I'm at the heart of the sky
Below, above, all around, sparkling stars move by!
It's dark as darkness but not void, solid like hills
On which flickering lights move crisscrossing
When villagers move searching the flock lost
Or, return from a late-night faraway fair
Darkness is the sky, vaporous clouds the Milky Way

On which fire-flies wink and dance like moving stars
Palpable yet unseen lie the vales and knolls of your body
My heart reaches out, behold, my star in my palm!

Still deep asleep but in supra-sensation of the heart
In the quiet night, I discern myriad of sounds
The beating of the heart, the tiptoe of the rain
The rustle of moist air, suppressed breathing of desire
The inaudible murmuring, whispering, and humming
Then thunder strokes, shafts of lightning, violent storms
Below the forest frenziedly tossing about and shrieking
Swelling streams, bursting dams, crescendo, inundation

I come, all is quiet, me lonely and alone
Above the sky is clear and ever so buoyant
Below lies blissed earth, disrobed, dishevelled, drenched
The spell is broken, Oh! You far, far away!

Youth and freshness what struck me as she entered
Truant wanders off a schoolgirl to sailors' den
Amidst rugged mountains one suddenly comes across
A tender flower, precariously dangling from the precipice

She was all eager yet not ready to give up girlhood
All ripe and ready yet hesitated to be a woman yet
Inconstant royalty of the same body to girl-woman
At your sweet will you were a bud or a flower

She wore a cotton shirt, white and half-sleeved
A light woollen tartan skirt in red and black
A pair of brown faded shoes of a schoolgirl
A fawn tiny leather bag slung across left shoulder
She was a student at the university

Wanted to volunteer herself for the project
She had all the qualifications, qualities
It was symbiosis in the workplace!

NOTES

1=Not this...not that, said with reference to God.
2=A god of fierce disposition, later day Shiv.
3=Self-born Manu, the originator of all human beings.
4=A great period of time. There are four yugs–Saty (1,728,000 years), Treta (1,296,000 years), Dvapar (864,000 years), and the present one, Kali (432,000 years). After each Yug destruction and creation takes place. After four yugs, great destruction and great creation take place, and the cycle of the four Yugs starts anew.
5=Hindu God who delivered Gita.
6=Milk-maidens of Gokul, the place where Krishn grew up.
7=The Primordial sound which is the origin of the universe.
8=The founder of Sikhism.
9=A river of North India.
10=A sort of pie, filled with vegetables (generally potatoes and peas, but now with other vegetables also, and with meat in non-vegetarian variety) and deep-fried. Now also popular in the West.
11=Indian bread is made of flour dough. For each bread, a small portion of the dough is to be flattened and spread in a circular form with a rolling pin. This then is baked on a hot iron plate. Both making the dough and then flattening individual pieces in circular form require quite a lot of practice.

Wooing

From the very first day, she picked up the work
And grasped fast whatever new there was to learn
She seemed perfect, never erring in whatever she did
She endeared herself to all without trying to

The computer is the same, the characters the same
Why her letters seem more elegant, more beautiful
The same flute gives different melodies in other hands
And the same words sound different on various lips

She smiled all the time, but knew to be serious
Cold as deep freezer, the chill deep down the bones
A door violently slammed and shut on the face
When her eyes went blank, the world stopped to exist

An evanescent smile, flicker of welcome in the eyes
Made a universe out of nothing, a dreamland
When those lips are pursed and eyes are steely
The whole universe tumbles down into a black hole

The *bonne ambience,* pride of doing one's best smiling
Being together all day, even on excursions outdoors
Encouraged me to joke and say nonsense nothings
Sometimes she seemed to understand, often as if jokes

She sat beside me, so near I could touch her
So near I could smell a living flower around
So near her far away look was mortal shock
So near she could stab me with her indifference!

A lonely cloud melting its heart over a desert
In vain! The rain never reaches the parched earth

The milk flows into the breasts, sucked in again
Ah! It's a dream, the babe is yet unborn

The ship has reached the dreamland, wandering's end
Finds nowhere to berth in the rocky seashore
Yet leaves not, it goes on round and round
Anchor it in here, or flounder on these rocks

The books are there, films and TV and video
My unfinished poem awaiting me in solitude
Friends invite me to drinks, dance and dinner
Weekend trekking or island hopping on a skinny boat

These fulfilled my life, why now they seem hollow
A flower without fragrance, a word devoid of meaning
Without you company is crowd, solitude desolation
Without you life is death, death only salvation

The rising sun gave the hope of seeing you
And when parting took away you with him
From day to day, from Monday to Friday
My heart has become a lotus, a sun-flower!

Then comes the weekend, the end of myself
Three full nights before I see you again
Two days in the bed thinking and dreaming of you
Roaming around in deserted rooms like *Ashwathama*[1]

It could have gone like this till eternity
I wonder how many lovers could not say
The three words they wanted to say most
And were separated by time, the words unspoken

When men are petty and selfish, women uncaring
When evil attracts evil leaving a good man lonely
When an unjust word, deed, pricks at the heart
And a deep melancholy wraps around the sorrow
When it rains or snows, shines or lights
The world seems too beautiful to be indoors
When without any seeming reason, in itself
The heart bursts out with infinite joy
Then to share that happiness with nature
Or to dissolve the pain in the beauty
I walk along a lonely trail or on the seawall
And forget the pain of sadness and joy

I loved roaming around Boulevard Den
The ambience of art and culture soothed me
Transported me to my heart's fond realms
Whatever else, at heart I am still a poet

From Den I walked along the Pirate Creek
Lined with motorboat bistros, drink, dine and drift
Across which lies lighted downtown
Reflected in calm waters a magic haunt of childhood

In dreamlike trance I hear, 'Good Evening, Sir!'
With a radiant smile she proffers her hand
Ah! A moment of reunion, separation for ages
A light touch like a soft kiss on drowsy cheeks
I say, with beating heart, what a surprise!
I live at Pirate Creek, just there, points she
Where I had come many times, just now too
She was all along so near, I searched far!
She invites me to her home, I say first you
Come to my house, then maybe I will

She smiles, she would come next day
Another smile, light handshake, and gone!

How does a priest await God at the temple
Does he adorn himself more or the shrine
Does he go out or receive at the portal
What he offers Him, flowers, fruits, prayers
How does a bride receive the groom on honeymoon bed
How to wait outside closed doors, cry of the newborn
How does a mother await her children from school
Wife, her man at dusk coming home from far away lands
How does the parched earth await the rains
The early hours the sun, twilight the moon
Cold and denuded trees, flowery dress
And butterflies and bees flowering buds

What will I say, how will I greet, when she comes
Will I shake hands or kiss her on the cheeks
For new advance, more intimacy, prelude to love
I practice words and deeds, nothing left to chance!

The house is dirty, I still unshaven, unbathed
The fridge is empty, what should I offer her
Is the outer gate open, does the doorbell ring
What if somebody else comes or telephones

I'm ready, house shining, fridge full
I go to door, sit, go to the window, peep out
Stand there, roam around, again go to the door
See the watch, pray to God, repeat it all!

I resolve to stand in front of the window
Till fifty pedestrians, no, only maidens espy I

All fails, I'm still at window, resolving again!
Only as long as fifty cars, Oh! No, cabs pass by

I count up to a thousand, slow after nine hundred
Last fifty a crawl, ten years, three eternity!
I try telepathy, my mental powers to charm her to me
Seek help from dark forces, unkind gods, all in vain!

A cab slows down, perhaps you in there
A girl appears at the bend, it's you!
The iron gate is rattling, did the bell ring
Heart jumps at each sound, half-wishing she never came!
It's morning, it's noon, evening, lo! It's night
I still await you, without eating, without relaxing
On the slightest stir, I open the door
Often the bell rings, there is none on the sill
Even at midnight, I lay awake awaiting you
I dream of you, know not, if drowsy or awake
Next day is Sunday, and I still await
Imprisoned in my home, in thoughts of you

You come to university as if nothing had happened
A curt 'Good morning, Sir' and you begin your work!
I swallow my pride, my tears, I'm patient
Let there be two worlds–office and home

So near yet so far, so dear yet so indifferent!
I wear my heart on my sleeve, she sees not
I feel so neglected and unwanted, I cry out loud
To hell with her, immediately I take my words back

In my desperation I lament
This girl has no heart

How could she be so indifferent?
To the cry of my lovelorn heart

How nothing affects her, touches her
She is like a lotus leaf
The torrential rain of my tears
Falls, falls, falls, flows away!

I endured the whole week, again it's Friday
I have to set my pride aside, otherwise
I would suffer another weekend in which
Perhaps you could have liked to come to me!

I ask about the last Saturday, you just shrug
But promise to come to me the next day
I imprison myself in my house, incommunicado
All alone with quivering body and thumping heart

You come not! That weekend, the next
The next, the next, for months together
Each Friday I invite you, you say yes
Yet you come not for several months!

In my simplicity and helplessness, I understand not
You never meant to come, you just said so
As one says things to an innocent child
Who believes in everything told by loved ones

In love you are always on the losing side
It's her sweet will to accept or reject
You could move mountains but the heart of Eve
Is moved by what forces, poor Adam knows not

Then one Friday she asks where exactly I live
As simply as this, as if nothing had happened
As if she had never told she would come
As if I had never awaited her at home!

My blood boils tears well up in my eyes
To hell with her, she is not the only one
Where is my pride, where my manly rage?
Why I submit to the whims and caprices of her?

Retreat? Never! But where to and how to advance?
In love boats are drowned and bridges burnt
Faced with a stony heart, a lover but can
Serenade all night and pray under her casement

Were love a war, I would storm the fortress
Go berserk, kamikaze attacks, ultimate sacrifice
By brawn or brain I would have won
All is fair in love and war!

All is fair in love and war?
In war maybe, but not in love
Love is showing white flag at the very first
A surrender of self, complete and unconditional
All means are unfair in love
Even love as a means for love is unfair
It's barter, quid pro quo, love is
Giving and surrendering, not plundering and winning
Love is to say I forfeit all my life
To you and for you, and if need be
I'll willingly forgo it without
Asking for a flicker of love in your eyes!

How helpless is a man in love!
It's real catch-22, a no-win situation
A bird without wings, a ship in storms
She herself is plaintiff, judge and executioner!

Yours not to defend, fight or run away
Not to surrender or beg pity and mercy
When wounded still keep on the vigil
And die unknown, unsung, at the post!

Two wandering stars may meet once again
A needle could be found in the stack of hay
But to win the love of indifferent Eve
Is slave to more chance and effort

Who said love respects the convention of reciprocity?
Year after year, receive I New Year cards
From those whom I never send, and await
In vain from those whom I love and remember!

Love alone is not enough, love is too fragile
A faux pas and the crystal ball is broken
Hold it tight, dies it of stifling and fright
Loose flies it away, never, never to return

One Sunday when the sun was approaching zenith
Shadowy hopes reduced to despair, then Phoenix
On the rocky seashore a wave shatters
Unmindful rushes forward another with suicidal frenzy

In the grey twilight of hope and despair
When the flowers are withered, buds still closed

I go up and begin to take a bath
At the most vulnerable, naked, drenched and foamy

It rings, two tentative and hesitant reluctant rings
Should I ignore? It's impossible to do so
(Though when together we did it time and again!)
All through this your thought never came to me!

Naked run I to outer room, peer through windowpane
My God! It's you, it's she, it's her
Don't go away! Wait! Run I to terrace?
Fool! You grabbed not even a towel, go back!

I almost stumble onto terrace naked through the door
And manage to convey through waving of a hand
I've heard and coming down to open
Don't go away thinking I am not at home!

Hurriedly I put on whatever came in handy
Stumbling, tumbling, slipping, run down the stairs
Open the door, the gate and mumble a welcome
Bring them in, yes, she was with a younger girl

Where are the books you promised says she
Upstairs, let us go to see and collect them
We go up, at last all alone are we two
Is it a sweet dream or still sweeter reality!

My mouth is dry, hands shaking, heart pounding
Standing near the bed I show her the books
Barely have I shown two or three that
An insane desire takes hold of me, Oh! Shame

Suddenly, I try to embrace and kiss you on the lips
You swerve and I get only a glancing touch
Evanescent touch, so swift, so fleeting, Ah! Eternity
Books fall on floor, on bed fall you, me O! Niagara

Nonplussed perhaps, not angry, even half-expectant
But I knew I had lost the game of love
Like a fielder in cricket who drops lollipop of a catch!
I turn, you pick-up books and go down

I sit down on the bed, head between hands
This is the end of months of patient wooing
What a folly, what lousy behave, what a weakness
Time enough to lament, go down she may leave

Quickly I change, hope you do not notice
You are sitting pretty as if nothing happened
After some time, 'We came directly from the church
Already we are late, let's go home'

You go, you come and go like a storm
Which comes out of nowhere and goes where
Leaves behind much debris and change also
We wonder why it came and why it went

You come and go like the rain, the snow
Flowers in the wild, falling leaves in the alley
A dream in the midst of sleep and waking
A smile on the face of a weeping child!

The moment I awaited so long and eager
Came and slipped by like a glistening fish

Will to wretched me she ever come again
And how will I face her tomorrow at work

What a shame if she tells all what happened
Is the end of love in ignominy and fall
All day, all night, all sorts of thoughts, nightmares
Outwardly was I calm but burning painfully inside

Next day lo and behold! She is all there
Working as usual as if nothing had happened ever
Immense relief and insane anger flood me together
And again the same desires, all resolves forgotten!

The week flies by as usual, it's again Friday
Pride and love wage the eternal seesaw battle
Reason wins at the end, why waste precious time
Very little time to love, none to waste on pride

Last week I could not offer even a glass of water
There is chilled beer awaiting you, will you come
I'll come after the church, says she simply
Oh! The relief, shower of dreams in fireworks display

Prompt comes she at the exact hour she came last
Thank God! This time she is quite alone
We sit and talk nothings for fleeting hours
How different is she from I knew so far

We drink not chilled beer but mellow French wine
How divine drinks taste when we drink together!
We prepare food, I more a hindrance than help
In a few hours we feel we were eternally together

She is not tipsy but I know all aflame
I could kiss her, but I'm happy to love her
How flies time, it's already beginning to get dark
How much I wish the time to stop forever!

Next week on Saturday she had a tutorial
As pre-arranged comes to me straight from there
Again on Sunday, and we wonder in our hearts
How could we live so long without each other!

We meet next week also, we are supremely happy
Something is missing, the happiness is incomplete
Eye in eye we seem to await who winks first
Two wills, two prides, wage an internecine war

Oh! Fool she has done more than her due
By coming to you alone, love's rules are strange
Her one wrong and one right may make all wrong
You did wrong, do it again, then all will be right!

You think she will kiss you first, never!
It would go on for eternity, be a man
Lead her by the hand, ever so little squeeze
She will dance fine, but first lead her on

Our day together passes in a wink
Why waste it on false egos
Let's love in a hurry, make most of it
God gave us abundant love but little time

Next week I whirl her around ever so gently
Her eyes sparkle like diamonds, her head jerks up

Our hands clasp each other, in frenzy lips meet
I had intended a swift kiss but the lips stuck!

Honey-dipped dew-draped rosebud yet closed
Misty cool breeze from cascading rainbow drops
Full moon autumnal caressing blessed embrace
All things sweet and soft, sensual and scarce!

Our lips press more, bodies entwine, limbs bind
Twin sabres stuck at point-blank, yet Oh! So soft
Our mouths open and tongues embrace each other
As if we two the medium, they true lovers!
We gasp for breath yet lips refuse to part
My hands wander but hers arrest them yet guide
That was a feint! Now my lips explore
Her forehead, eyes, nose, cheeks, ears and chin
Like a runner who runs faster than his legs carry
Stumbles and falls flat on the face all bruised
The burning passions consume already aflame bodies
We fall on the sofa too bewildered, too fulfilled

Like some unconscious sensation arising from
Multitude of perceptions and passions
I remember the touch of her unimaginably soft body
To believe, I touch her again, Oh! The velvety touch

Just a kiss and the change, the metamorphosis in her
Her face was softer, hallowed, eyes aflame, lucid
And full of sweet, sweet, overwhelming love for me
Her soul at peace with herself and the whole world

When the fierce battle is stopped for the night
Arms are laid, wounds washed and bandaged

Then in the calm of night one thinks of it
His pains, his joys, his blessing of being alive

When the tumultuous storm of passions is passed
Fire in the body doused, heart at peace in itself
She is gone, lie I wallowing in my joys and pains
I relive the first kiss, Ah! My changed life

Like a dulcet melody, a mellow memory
Which lingers on forever in the heart
I carry infinite sweetness of that first
First-ever kiss till today on my lips!

Before I was in a hurry to consummate our love
Now that I won the first kiss, I was content
As a mountaineer sitting at the base camp
Sure that one day he will scale the summit
But we did advance, from kissing to petting
Then we did discard clothes one day
Ah! With what to compare, equate her body
Which God made sensuous, soft and sweet

How foolish is man, thinks face is all the body
It's just the tip of the iceberg, mere one-ninth
Many a love-boat has foundered, dreams shattered
Knowing not what lies covered, what the folds hide
Earth is beautiful but the essence lies deep down
All the gems–diamond, ruby, sapphire, plenteous more
Reservoirs of cold and hot waters, gushing up at will
And fire and lava and mad tremors shaking it all
Face expresses with fake aids, light, tears and smiles
What happens outside it, which is felt by the body

Body reveals directly what it feels, undergoes
Oh! World, cover the face, keep the body bare!

Thousands of things happen together, at random
Passions and emotions, love and sex, new discoveries
The storyline gets blurred and thin, time non-linear
What came first, what next, did all come together?

Things must have happened to me in some order
In some cause and effect sequence, in progression
Looking back lovelorn I find all jumbled up
All memories eager to bestir at once

Let me not be ashamed, it's not my story alone
But of countless others, of the humanity
If my virtues show through, let my foibles too
I'm above them now, even uncaring, unashamed

Her body found I soft yet hot as bed of embers
Which burnt me oft times till I learned the secret
Of a fire dancer, the fear is in the head, not act
Confidence and one could dance till fires are doused

She loved dancing and danced heavenly like fairies
I was awkward, body stiff, ears unmindful of music
Two great regrets in life, music and dance, alas!
Loved both, tried hard, Ah! Some things are by birth

Yet when I danced with her and followed her cue
(Male chauvinists we all, must she dance attendance)
We danced perfectly, I enjoyed, what's more, she too
Dancing, how easy it is, just follow the partner!

Often she danced with others who asked, 'May I'
Seeing her dancing I never felt pang of jealousy
Later much later I did not mind anything at all
If it were what she wanted and was happy about

How happy one feels knowing full well in the heart
Whatever she may dance, with whomsoever
In the dimmed lights, mellowed music, hearts fast
The slow dance is for me and me alone!
All may shake hands, some may even kiss at cheeks
But the luscious lips are for me and me alone
She may talk, laugh, even dine and dance with all
The bare body and night are for me and me alone
Who could take away that slow dance, kiss on lips
Not riches, not kings, not even multitude of gods
If by ruse or force they are taken, body violated
Who could abuse and ransack my love in her heart
Is it the same dance forced upon the paralyzed feet
The same kiss thrust upon unwilling dry sealed lips
If love could be bought, could be forced
How much the poor and weak would have suffered!

We did all, the names of which I learned later
There was no shame in it, it came from nature
Still in my Eden was the forbidden ripe fruit
Which she ever refused, does Eve tempt or stop

Some primitive instinct in a woman, many men too
Of sacred sacrifice, wholesome offering to love
On the great ritual day, amidst invocations and incense
Delay the ultimate surrender, even if loving and willing

I love you, I'm yours, this body is yours
Love it, take it, use it, as you wish
It's a sin, sacrilege, it's for who says 'I do'
If it be you, otherwise I'm a spinster for life!

I blackmail, your love is wanting and distrustful
Embracing and kissing, I press at her naked heart
If it be a proof of love, you suffer without it
I too want to give and have, Oh! Let's do it all
She closes her eyes, not like a sacrificial lamb
Not as a sobbing child before the painful prick
But in utter surrender, the culmination of love
In eager hope of the pleasures and pains of sex

The cup brimming with the milk of human passions
Tilt I to her proffered lips, and then pull away
Like a hovering bee sits lightly on blossoming buds
Then buzzes off before the bud splits into a flower

How vulnerable, how pathetic one becomes in love
Virtuous women and wise men are led astray by it
Open-eyed they walk up to and fall into the pit
Still think they are lying on the bed of flowers

Here she lies naked with trusting heart, closed eyes
Who is most virtuous, upright, wise in worldly ways
Lying to family and friends, skipping her Sunday church
Oh! How easily could one be duped in the name of love

How easy it is to simulate love, fake it
By a few smiles, deep sighs and sly looks
Love declarations, tender kisses, warm tears
From love to sex, rejection and oblivion

The love in surrendered body, closed eyes
I'll not take by guile or force, less in love more in sex
In tumultuous tossing, tumbling, frenetic groping, clasping
In maddening hurry, in too desperate, culmination

Little by little, more and more, things came with her
Dresses, underclothes, shoes, and all feminine presence
Little by little I started visiting her house, her family
Our love's progress was at the worldly level too

First she came only weekends, then weekdays too
First she came for a few hours, then stayed late nights
Then occasionally over-night, supposed to be with friends
Later, all pretensions lost, she practically lived with me

First I waited outside, then was welcome in for tea
From there I progressed to dinner table, then late nights
From down-stairs to up-stairs took time, as reverse in sex
Then we had our own room, in her house too

NOTES

1=Son of *Guru Dronachary*, he was one of the three main survivors of *Mahabharat* war from the *Kaurav* side. He promised dying *Duryodhan*, the *Kaurav* king, that he would kill the *Pandavs*. The three of them entered the Pandavs camp in the night when *Pandavs* were elsewhere. *Ashwathama* killed the five children of *Draupadi* mistaking them for five *Pandavs*. Later, after a showdown between *Arjun* and *Ashwathama*, Krishn cursed him to roam the earth for 3000 years infested with wounds.

Loving

Then came her birthday long-awaited, last of teens
I was well aware but feigned as if ignorant
Quietly that Friday afternoon, I said, 'Good Night'
Never once I asked her to come on weekend!

But promptly in the evening just before dinner time
Knocked in my best suit, hiding flowers and the gift
Of the dress which many a time had she espied
At The Mall with coveted glances, quiet sighs

We did not go to our little cosy nightclub
But to the five-star hotel overlooking the sea
Oft-times she had hinted me to take her there
The best I had saved for the memorable day

She was dressed in my gift, in all bridal white
A tilting red hat and a redder rose on the heart
It was that moment, that day, comes to every woman
When she is the most beautiful girl in the universe

We entered the hall, a gaping hush fell around
Women were jealous of her, men envious of me
If women could they would have lynched her
Men grabbed and taken her away from me!

It was hard for women to mask the inadequacy felt
Harder for men to hide lustful glances from them
How good it feels sometimes to be aware of
The covetous glances of all upon what you possess!

It was her day, we had to go by her desire
I forgot my strong scotch, we drank mellow Burgundy

Me a vegetarian, still she ordered all non-veg
(Was it the beginning of the pleasures of flesh for me?)

That day the band seemed to play only for us
(They did play 'Happy Birthday to You' for her)
We danced every dance giving nobody no chance to
Pilfer and share ever so little which was only ours

Very late we returned home, she clinging to me
We entered my room, promptly she swooned in my arms
Night was young, it was her night, my night too
The master of tender surprises was at its best

For in the room I had prepared the bridal bed
Heaps of soft petals of white jasmine and red roses
With canopy of marigolds, festoons of lilies
In flowers on flowers was written, "I Love You, Dearest!"

We sank as one into flowers, moon in dense clouds
Kissed, fondled, disrobed each other in frantic hurry
We were anointed as King and Queen of Love
By the smearing of flowers on our naked bodies
We fought on the opposite sides for the same cause
I drew the first blood, but then she retaliates
With thrusts, cuts and bites, we fight unto death
And in the deadly duel end up clasped together
Violent storm rages, screaming winds blow unabated
It's cloudburst, it rains all night heaps of torrents
Rivers swell and dams burst, then all is calm
In love washed ashore we lie huddled together
She opens her bright eyes, smiles, kisses me tenderly
'Oh, dearest!' Entwined swoons with a beatific smile

Seeing her blissfully happy, I feel blessed too
Is there anything else in life after this night!

I stir not lest her sweet dream be broken
Yet I might have dozed off, she is waking me
Dressed in the spare dress she had kept with me
It's still dark outside but she is ready to leave
'I must go, my sister will let me in'
'It's already too late, what difference does it make'
But reasons of Eve are difficult to fathom, just obey
Still smelling of flowers we are on the dark road

I deposit her, go to sleep, dream of her
I'm still dreaming when she really comes back
With a bag 'We are supposed to go out of town'
For the whole weekend, we leave not the flowery bed!

We made love, lay silent in the explicit embrace
Talked and kissed and excitedly again came to it
Two blessed souls on long pilgrimage to shrine of Cupid
The first lovers in the Garden before the serpent misled

The doorbell rings often, telephone more than usual
The sun pines away for moon, she ambles through stars
Many rounds they make, many rains, snow and falls
Many Ages pass, many *Yugs,* Annihilations and Creations

This bed is our universe, acts of love creations
On it armies of passions fight uncertain battles
How much *Prakriti*[1] hid, why *Purush*[2] stirred her
All's yours, love and sex, I'm just prime mover

The three *Guns*[3] were in just equilibrium in you
All the materiality for many individual worlds
All active yet inert till I fathomed the depth
And created my own cosmos, call it real or unreal

I thought her *Miss Correct All, Miss Right Always*
Which had it not been for her charm and smiles
Is difficult to love, even if difficult to condemn
To be human and loveable one has to err and sin

Before all this, I had thought her to be
Loveless, sexless, passionless, beautiful figure in wax
Cursed God for wasting feminine sex and beauty
Who suspecting Greek gift returns unopened, unseen

Here she was showing me what love is made of
Leading me to ecstasy of orgasmic sex repeatedly
Do tender passions in any heart stir as in her
Oh! The abundance of love, sex and desires in her!

For almost one year I was with her all-day
Thinking of her, loving her in erotic dreams
Yet I knew nothing of her, all mere facts only
Real her remained all hidden and elusive to me

So do the world, life and God remain obscure to us
The more peer intently, the more we perceive nothing
In a moment of happy communion, divine revelation
Or by intuitive grasping, we comprehend the reality

To millions of us poor that moment comes never
To those whom it comes know not how to say it

We understand not, disbelieve or laugh at them
Perhaps my fate is same yet I'm born obstinate

Monday comes flying, she readies herself to go
First to home, then to varsity where we meet again
A couple of hours' separation, Oh! How long
When life is made of only a few winks

Many byes we said, many times kissed and embraced
Oft-times she went to the door, returned for the last kiss
Many times we embraced against the door, I opened it
Only to pull her in again for some forgotten final kiss!

Never say Good Night to a lover leaving him alone
To toss and tumble lonely in the bed all night
It's killing to be together all night then separate
Oh! Never say Bye to a lover early in the morn

From the bridal bed she took a lily, me a rose
That rose is still fragrant in the album of memories
More loquacious than the whole lot of photos
And redder, redder than our lonely bleeding hearts

The bridal gown was splattered with all the colours
Of the flowers of the consummation night of our love
She took the battered hat, me flower drenched dress
As souvenir of the night which needs no souvenirs

The love flowers we collected in the bridal sheet
Later set afloat in afternoon glimmering Lovers Bay
Where they floated and flowed like spreading fire
To the sea unbroken between your country and mine
In a couple of hours we meet again

Same curt 'Good Morning, Sir,' reserved mien
How good is a woman in hiding love and womb
Man wears his heart out on his sleeve

Seeing her so near yet far, genial but so aloof
I had a mad impulse to tell the whole world
This girl is mine, what the heck! I love her
Yet more than her, I hid it from the world

Yet much was changed in her, some obvious to all
Her face was more radiant, eyes more sparkling
The faint shadow of care was now a mellow sheen
She was no longer a girl, though yet not a woman

I could discern fleetingly as frolicking fish
In her eyes when they fixed on me stealthily
Desperate love and longing in her for me
Hidden though like fire in the heart of earth

They say the fruit of patience is sweet
Poor preachers never knew how sweet it could be
Days, weeks and months flew by as if few winks
We remained ensconced in our haven of love

We made love to the fill of our hearts
Yet they remained as unfulfilled as ever
The more we loved, the more we made love
The more we made love, the more we loved

We wanted to efface time and space by our love
We made love at all times–dusk, dawn, day and dark
Every room, every corner of our house knew our love
Even sofa, table and shower are our close confidants

Oh! The preponderance, the abundance of sex in love
Wild horse running berserk, unseating the rider
The sun shines the moon, still she eclipses him
Bewitches more, so does naked sex simulating love

From first kiss to last emiss it's sex all the way
When the beloved is missing it's the body which pines
And pining and searching sends love as a Trojan Horse
When all the world is sleeping, raids in the dark

Topless towers tumble, flames reach sky high
Passionate armies clash violently in the dark
Thrust and push, push and thrust, warm blood
Love and sex both come together with a shriek

Whatever reserve of forces I summoned to my aid
I knew it was an unequal war between the sexes
She stoops to conquer, submits to overwhelm
Yields to penetrating thrust only to overpower

Dancing with her all those dances did help
I knew the subtlest cues of her eloquent body
To abandon my self to her whims and fancies
And then to be one with her soul and heart

I could see it in the mystic glow of her face
Or the feverish touch of her soft body
The subtle change in the aroma of her fragrance
The nude dance of her body's shameless desires

The self-defeating backbreaking iron grip
The obscenities, shrieks, storms in the gasps

Spasmodic quicksand, incessant crashing waves
Caving in of the shore, all inundations, all calm

Nymphet nympho opens her eyes, smiles, kisses
Entwines me in her limbs and slips into sleep
With a half-formed smile on the tender lips
Oh! God, how happy is she, how blessed me

Sometimes distracted banks cave-in by earth's tremors
Or incessant rain breaks them before the river swells
Wave after wave of gushing waters shriek oh...hhh!
And subside in mellowed expanse of yielding banks

My heart sobbing behind a tree, chipped toy in hands
A proud new possession, now unwholesome offering
She'd first disdain then condescend, wantonly break
For some slight, some defect, my toy, her divine right!

She lies fidgeting, tossing around, not sleeping a wink
A smouldering fire sprawling across a barren patch
Like Shylock, she would demand her pound of flesh
In love she was generous, in sex hard taskmistress!

The sky pours his heart out, earth receives gratefully
The more he gives, the more she returns, both blessed
Greedy sky sometimes takes, gives not, parched earth
Lucky us, we loved and our bodies sexed each other

She loved violently, scratching and biting
Sometimes her lips clasped bruising the skin
Once she bruised all my face with her kisses
For a week I remained at home blaming hot oil!

She was unsparing in love, but spoiled me later
Preparing native foods, revamping the house
At times even redoing the clothes and utensils
All seemed dirty to her what was done by me

She spoiled me, but I spoiled her all the more
More than a mother spoils her only son
Her wish was my command, be it a whim or fancy
At home, she was the queen, me a humble slave

I prepared bed tea and brought it hot to her
Then kissed away slumber from her drowsy body
I pulled her on my lap and put the cup to her lips
Weekends she slept again or we loved once more

When she gets up again, I put sandals on her feet
And carry her still half-asleep to the bathroom
From where she promptly evicts me, no dear there
When the door clicked again I carry her to the bed

She sipped another tea, I read Morning Star to her
Gave her a shower or bath, our favourite love haunt
We ate in the bedroom sitting on the ground
The first bite, first spoonful, I always offered her

Dinner was cooked together with weekend drinks
Often got too drunk to eat much what we prepared
It was still better than at the beginning of love
Too busy, too early at love had no time for dinner

I carried her up, but no amount of drinks
Would make her forget what she was wont to do

She took a shower, cleaned teeth, brushed hair
Anointed her body, came to bed fresh as a bud

While I awaited in the bed, only mildly impatient
From student days things refreshing–tea or shower
Were for me to ward off sleep for whole night study
She tried to convert me, me her, both remained zealots

We talked long and explored each other's body
A thing of beauty is not slave to novelty
A rainbow, a lake, a mountain are always beautiful
Her beautiful body yet, was new and novel each night

'Stop!' Said temptress Circe with alluring smile
Who could stop the wanderlust of wild passions
The terrain is mine, go I to Red Canyon land
One hand arrests my finger, other pulls me to her!

She leads astray the wandering hands and mouth
Then arrests them for greater pleasures of flesh
The violent storm and gushing floods shake me
Up-rooted and flown away I plunge in eddying waters

Sometimes she slept soon, some nights lay awake
I caressed her and scratched her head till she slept
Only to wake, again to demand what was perfect
Or to carry on from where I had left unfinished

Dear! In loving you, I have become a mother!
I suckle you, put to sleep with caresses, kisses
Tickling you on the head and talking in lullabies
You scream and howl if I sleep before you
Sometimes you're still hungry, breasts are suck

In tantrum, you squeeze and bite flaccid nipples
I put a finger in your mouth, you are calm
More than the milk, you need the sucking
Some days you're sick, others only a little hungry
Pull your lips away when the breasts are still full
It hurts, it hurts so much, I squeeze out the milk
Or in dream I suckle you, morn wet blouse

You too see dreams of plenty of milk overflowing
And move your lips in sleep and hug me
You put your mouth to my breasts, they harden
Oh! Wherefrom over-flows so much love for you

Yet I had my share of irrationality and stupidity
She was nearly always with me yet I was jealous
The moment she was out of my sight
I thought of suitors galore wooing her!

It had taken me a year to win her over
And she had given herself so completely to me
Ignoring her family, friends, even church, still
I feared even shadow of other men over her path

But now far away wallowing in my sweet pain
I peer through the window and see you blest
Asleep in alien embrace and tip-toeing retreat
Lest you follow me, abandoning your paradise

If I was jealous she was thousands of times more
She censored letters, smelled and checked clothes
Forbade me to talk to or even see anything feminine
Walking together censored even my wandering gaze!

Jealousy was like, perhaps it was the same
Fear of losing each other, soaked deep into bones
Like a man in dark forest fears each corner
And sees terrible things where there are none

How ironic, it was not somebody
Who came between us and separated
It was our love which stood like a wall
And put us on either side of it!

Yet if we feared losing one another so much
And both loved each other above life
Why we fought constantly on every issue
When there was no cause, we still fought on

Oh! The endless, pointless, discussions, so futile
By the end we forgot who was on which side!
We fought on mere trifles, felt hurt deeply
Took revenge by trying to hurt still more

Some fights were, which are and always will be
Between husbands and wives who love each other
Each trying to reform the other, in vain
And chiselling out the other in one's own image

She wanted me to be as punctilious as she was
Shave daily, don't put on the same dress twice
Why you scatter your clothes all over the room?
What's this dirty wet towel doing on the bed?

I obeyed only immediately to disobey her
And in her discomfort and grumbling found

The joys of being the master of the house
Till she threw me out of the chaotic room

Yet I did not understand why she cared not
For the profound things, I tried to teach her
Changed subject, went to the kitchen or fell asleep
When I talked of classics and philosophy!

Oh! Dear, now I don't fight, don't argue
Shave daily, put on fresh clothes, your colours
Keep my shoes shining and hair trim and proper
And in each thing remember you and weep

When love is so great, so all-consuming
It's hurt by love which is a bit less
To prove we're not hopelessly in love
To reassure our panicky hearts, we love and fight

We loved love only and kept lots of it
Buried deep down into our heart of hearts
Yet apprehensive asked each other to keep vigil
Accused each other of falling asleep and fought

We fought for small things, for nothings
Yet the fights were bitter, to the end
Which needed only a word, a kiss, an embrace
To mend what we thought was broken forever

We did stop talking, meeting or having sex
But our love was love too short on time
We had wasted many days, we have but a few
Why waste even a wink of it on false egos

How could I not talk to her sitting so near
Or let another weekend pass without loving
When we had only numbered days together
So even the longest fights ended on Fridays

Love brought out the best in her
Only the worst in me, too shameful
To all others, I was kind, forgiving
For each offence of her, I took revenge

We were kissing and petting when suddenly
On something trivial, nothing at all, I flared
Hissed it's finished, it's finished, it's finished
And banging the door ran out of the beach hut
In the dead of night, in bitter wintry cold
She ran after me bare feet, almost naked
In a cotton night-gown, nothing under or over
As *Savitri*[4] might have run after *Yam*[5]
I walk fast and she runs after sobbing
Knowing if I reach the car, I'll go away forever
She caught me and clung to me like a bridal train
I dragged her till I felt her go limp
She was cold and shivering, fell upon me
I kissed her, she whispered, 'Love me'
On that desperate night, we made love
Of all things, on an upturned, ancient boat!
It was a love where bodies hardly mattered
And knew not what went through them
The souls communed with each other
And reassured and consoled sad love
She formed inaudible words with tender embrace
'Dear never be angry with me; never leave me;
I'm yours forever, treat me as you will'

In exhaustion or in bliss, she passed out
Here lies she on an upturned boat
A mermaid out of water in dark and cold night
Senseless, halfdead, half-mad, utterly alone
Who wagered all in love against loaded dice

Oh! Egotist, this, this you wanted to see
This, this you wanted to make her fall to
You were out to crush her, crush her pride
To swell and pamper your wretched ego
You needed to prove you're not helpless in love
Can live without her, without love, without sex
Like Buddh you can leave in the dark, leave all
Why not then you leave her now senseless and go
You were dying to see her run after you
And weep and plead and efface herself
You wished to play God, be the master of the house
Be true male chauvinist, make female into a slave

What love has done to her, made her so helpless
She belongs not now to family, world or God
With church plays truant, with world hide-and-seek
Love has butchered her, she sacrificed for love

That love I exploit, blackmail that love I
I go deeper than body and rape her soul
I lured, I kidnapped, I eloped with your love
A ponce, I send all the evils your way

In dark, bare feet and half-naked, I make you
To run the gauntlet of drunkards, druggists and pros
At a time when the town is filled with
Kidnapers and murderers and sex maniacs

I had thought of on that first day
'Truant wanders off a schoolgirl to sailors' den'
Oh! No, I've done worst, unpardonable
A schoolgirl sent nude to prisoners' cell

And now she lies here to be thought as
A hooker whosoever sees her in this state
As a man I may be ignored, let off
She is vulnerable to infamy, rape and murder

I believe in God as transcendent power
Not as somebody with hands and mouth and ears
I go to temple to pay my respects to religion
Hardly believing there is a God in there

But with you, I'll go to church on Sundays
To return what I stole from Him and you
Do they allow non-Christians to confess?
I'll confess all my sins of love

She shivered, I wrapped her up in my jacket
And carried her, as a groom carries his bride
On the nuptial night to the honeymoon bed
She slept on all night, that was our last fight

We were happy together, we stayed indoors
Then the temptress nature lured us out
We went all around the city, in nature's lap
Parks, forests, beaches, trails, and coves

National Park was nearest, we went time and again
Sat in cool bowers or under the sunny sky

Walked all around Seawalk, sat hours on beaches
Watching boats, ships, expanse of glittering water

Our favourite haunt was Sunset beach
We claimed it for ourselves, jealously guarded it
Never sharing it with colleagues and friends
Going together to the Campfire Fest on New Year Eve

As beauty is in the body, not in the face
Real country is the countryside not downtown
Sky is not moon only, it's expanse of stars
A country is rivers, hills, forests and beaches

Love searches new avenues to express, sex to do
They go out of the body, out of the heart
To the lap of Nature and find there
That freedom without which both are stifled

It was a National Day long weekend
When the days are sunny and bright and long
We went to your ancestral home out of town
It was our first far-out odyssey together

When desires re-stir and grope for the warm body
Leaving behind the fragrant warmth she slips away
Thrusting a pillow in my embrace, what devilish mind
When will the fair sex set their priorities right!
Still supremely happy with her loving parting gift
Half asleep I listen to that chatterbox talking
Through clatter of pots, rushing water, hissing kettle
Till I hear her coming up unsuspecting with teapot

Tit for tat, I arrange the pillows and cover them
She comes and tells them to get up for tea!
Uncovers, betrayed throws those soft missiles at me
In a tangle of limbs we fall on the bed

Just when she was at the point of surrender
Blasted cooker shrieks in protest in the kitchen
'My potatoes are boiling,' She flies away
What about me burning, Oh! Priorities, young lady

Yet I'm blissfully happy, sip my tea smiling
I know my love, it needed no sex
But to give love which would keep her
In that tipsy humour called bliss of love

Basking in that glow of love, she would uncover
And lie naked like nymphet nature long ago
Beaconing me with half-opened eyes, leading
My wandering fingers to the land of Erehwon

We enter the realm of undulating lands
Like huge sand dunes in vast desert expanse
With tall golden grass, bright young trees
Serpentine road like blazing trail of a long caravan

Each bend opened a fresh vista to explore
We wanted to stop and lie down under the sun
Far from nowhere, amidst the grass, a few flowers
Unknown, unlamented, like a lonely forgotten tomb

Yet I fervently prayed the journey never to end
Together and happy we drive on to eternity

The infinite expanse of grassland under golden sun
Amid excitement and wonder we reached our destination

It was beautiful from the road but was like
Gazing at firmament from the casement of cubicle
Away from the centre of the celestial dome
Sheltered from the shower of misty beamlets

I stand amidst undulating lands of golden grass
As might a fish at the surface of wavy sea
Shafts of sunshine stuck still in the stilled senses
A shiver swaying and spreading sinuous waves to eternity

Here and there young shiny trees stood in bunches
Dryads sunbathing and doing their faces
Swaying and bending and turning to see beautiful body
Flashing the looking-glass upon each other and me

Our bags we tossed to a nymphet who caught smiling
And tumbled down the slope unrolling golden carpet
We lay supine, still like a bird hovering on sun rays
Gazing at distant blue sky through golden haze

We lay under the warm sun, over-powering desire
Oh! God, I'm supremely happy, let me die!
Since I met you, this death wish comes to me
Again and again, as if there's no life beyond you

Together we went up only to roll down again
We made toboggans of boughs and pulled each other
Laughing and often tumbling down, rolling together
Till we found in sex catharsis of our happiness

Lengthening shadows and colder breeze reminded us
Of the passing time and we burst into laughter
When together we always lost count of time
Breakfast became lunch, lunch dinner, dinner lost

We took tea and some snacks and as planned
Entered the village in the dim darkness of dusk
'If they saw us, all would come to greet us
Let's have at least the first night to us'

The house was at the foot of surrounding hillocks
Screened from other similarly positioned houses
On the first were a veranda and two big rooms
All dark and wrapped in antiquity and solitude

We went up crumbling stone steps and opened
A dark room with uneven surface and cluttered
With utensils and a cot and some dry wood
The lantern was sprawling on the floor all-empty

We put some wood in the hearth and kindled fire
Bundled a few splinters and made a torch
In the precarious light of it fetched some water
From a trickle of a stream under a mango grove

It was quiet outside, full moon in the sky
In the absolute calm of night, it came to us
We two are all alone in the whole universe
Which is the Curse or Bliss of the Original Sin
There's nothing outside us, outside our love
Nothing, absolutely nothing, nothing at all
Even time is nothing, this night *déjà vu*
We even know what we will do or say next

We sat for long time till she flashed a smile
'We will again forget the dinner, I must
Feed you, as you are guest in our home'
Oh! Dear how cruel a guest proved I to you!

And she produced from our bags various things
Rice and lentils and vegetables, spices, even fruit
'Thief! When did you steal all these things'
'When you were busy arranging pillows to dupe me'!

We both prepared dinner, me helping her where
She needed none but out of love said nothing
She had not forgotten even the big metal plate
In which we both used to eat together

She surprised me by offering the first morsel
'My grandmother used to offer to her dead husband
We used to make fun of her, but now I know
She loved him as much as I love you'

I lay down on the floor near the fire
Seeing the play of flames on her naked body
While she moved around the room busily
And came to me to lie down near me

Next morning we went around the houses
As daughter and son-in-law of the village
This much love I never received in my country
How fortunate are some, how undeservedly lucky

Then we flew to our sunny grasslands
To lie down on our backs under the sky

We prepared lunch on a slab of rock
Sat together till the lengthening of shadows

In the evening all the villagers came to us
They made a bonfire and we danced around it
On the beats of drums which haunt me till today
Like an incessant insistent Come, Come, Come again

Past midnight they went, we sat peering into fire
'We'll lose each other, we'll separate'
In a trance looking vacantly into the fire
Said she voice of finality and unalterable fate

I feared her in such state and dreaded her words
She said 'I'm the medium; the voice comes from God'
In others I scoffed such super-natural things
In her I believed each word as gospel truth

What can one say in the face of finality
Her face mellows and I know now it's heart
'Still it's wonderful, it's bliss, it's heaven
For your love, I could endure eternal separation'

Oh! Dear it's your love which is wonderful
I know not how to love, just imitate
It's now only when I've understood your love
That I began to know how to love

'Do you know what those drums were for
It was the beat of the celebration of nuptials
And now they have left us for the consummation
Of marriage under the fire in traditional custom'

'If you make love to me, you'll lord over me
If I make love to you, I'll love you always
Let me make love to you, let me love you'
And under the sky, under the fire, she did

My surprise, my love, my sex, of the bed of flowers
Is as small to this love as nothing to infinity
Flames on her frenzied body, leaping fires inside me
Gazing the starry sky I lay as if under the rains

Her firm breasts, erect, quivered ever so slightly
As quiver and leap up a fire burning bright
It was a-quiver all, inside out, fire, grass, stars
In a desperate embrace all four came together

And then all was still, silence, not a stirring
The fire, wind, grass, distant drums and stars
All emotions, all desires, our bodies, our hearts
Perhaps they ticked again, we're still in that moment

Without moving she went to sleep as was her wont
Daring not to move under her I lay awake
What a quirk of evolution, ego or jumbled fights
Man won battle of sexes and lost war of ecstasy!

Man still thinks love is a wrestle mania
Where grabbing by hands and pinning down by body
Some sham strokes, mighty heaves, all sound and fury
A counterfeit victory, a feigned loss, goes for sex

After this love it's sacrilege to move in
Or to cover bodies by anything made by man

We slept under the stars beside the bonfire
On the bed, under the cover, of tall grass

Oh! The preponderance, abundance of love in sex
Pure spirit writhing in pain to express in form
Which is beyond expression, attributes, qualities
Both then continue the eternal duality paradox

Love is something to be learned by heart
And once learned, it's hard to forget
In work, in play, frivolous pursuits, even in opiates
Body and mind may be numbed; heart steadfast!

Love is learned by heart, also by mind and body
Pursuit of beloved, carnal knowledge, whims of fancy
Twilight to midnight oil even beyond in the dark
Try to grasp elusive, unstable form and content

Love and sex are coupled together
Like the word and its meaning
What came first, what last
What's greater, all foolish logicality
They are one like soul and God
God and world, matter and spirit
We separate them and not find a word
A single word for love and sex, sex and love
When we feel it's love, when act sex
When hearts talk it's love
When bodies explore it's sex
In the end both are the same, two names

While you are still learning, you have to love too
To give in abundance what her body craves

Love is giving, giving, giving only never grabbing
Man needs so little, can give infinite bliss

And when the body is tired, eyes heavy with sleep
Still to love, to kiss, talk, fondle, cajole
A slave to get up before the mistress, sleep after
To love is slavery, bonded labour, still so welcome

Hamlet's challenge is right, I go a step further
Thousands of mothers' love cannot equal my love
She gives the breasts to several children, to father
I give whatever is mine only to you, and only you

She loved surprises and I loved springing them up
Bed of roses, a rosebud with morning tea
A bar of chocolate kept in the purse unknown
Always together still send a love letter by post

I noted what she fancied, what she desired
Presented to her hidden in unexpected places
Under her pillow, in her drawer, in her pockets
A Valentine in her Bible, benevolent God smiles!

When she shouted for her clothes after a shower
I surprised her with a new dress much-coveted
'Happy anniversary of the day we first kissed'
We kissed, went under the shower again!

She wanted to take me to some remote island
I acted as if I cared not much for them
Then bought tickets for the Inner Islands
And packed things without telling the destination

It was a dream journey through dreamlands
Through sunny tracts and dark cold night together
In each other's embrace in each other's lap
A day and night passed as if in winks

Time and again she kept on pleading, I refusing
To rent a beach cottage at least for one night
'It's too costly, let's stay in some cheap motel'
She hated me as a wife hates a miser husband!

We arrived, my pilot friend was awaiting me
We made a round of the city in his helicopter
Then we flew straight to his private island
A star in between crescent moon seashore

He left and she flew into feminine rage
'Cheat, liar, fraud, impostor, I hate you'
I don't understand this girl, O! My God
I offer her Dream-time, not even 'Thank you'!

The island had everything which money could buy
House, car, boat, gadgets, food, drinks, beds
What else man needs if he had all these things
But do I really need them when I'm with you

The island has everything which nature can offer
Serene sky, sun, sand, sea, surf, and solitude
Are these not enough for us to live and love
With you do I still need this mundane world

We threw keys of the house on the roof
And our things and clothes in a corner

We would not touch any of those things
Would roam around the island all naked!

We were now at the mercy of Mother Nature
Without food, clothes, shelter, even a matchbox
And would remain so for our entire stay
Is love greater than life or a part of it

She was carefree but I was a bit apprehensive
If I fail in the first act, all will be spoiled
But it was hot and dry and I had no difficulty
Lighting a fire from two cobbles and grass

Rest was easy, even fun, how simple is life
We had fresh water, we had saltwater
Coconuts and palms, seafood and roots
How soft is the bed of sand under starry cover

Stars shower golden glitter which float down
On the wings of moonshine and alight lightly
As fall flakes of snow on spongy white earth
Kisses, murmured endearments, autumnal memories

We slept on the beach on a palace of mound of sand
Alone far, far away from all, all alone together
We rarely come together unless we run away, be far
From this madding crowd, from this mundane world

We drank coconut water and caught fish
Made our own hut out of palm fronds
Swam and frolicked and lay under the sun
Till the sea became all red like my love

Next night we went on boating and stopped
In the middle of sea between town and island
The sea was a-glimmer under full moon and stars
And the land had thousands of leaping bonfires

Amidst rolling sea and drums we lay awake
In the rolling boat making precarious love
Dancing shadows and leaping fires making motifs
On glimmering waters and our bodies astir

Third night we rowed out to sea, away, away
Till we lost land, were engulfed by immensity
Never were we so far far away from the world
Never we felt so nearer to each other than then

In the morn we found us swept away
Still farther into the sea, lost, completely lost
Yet we accepted the end calmly, even with relief
Great consolation, we'd be together until the end

How meaningless and absurd was our last worry
'What a shame we found together, dead, all naked!'

Perhaps this thought spurred us to action
We rowed by the light of the rising sun

We knew if we missed our island we're dead
Yet dying seemed going to sleep in embrace
After loving, loving so much, to the fill
We had lived so fully, we regretted nothing

Living with you, living loving you, that's life
Dying with you, dying loving you, that's death

In between all is nothing, meaningless nothing
Some illusion, some fake smiles and tears

We rowed leisurely knowing full well in our hearts
It's not the speed but direction which mattered
By midday, we did not come across the land
And knew that we're on the wrong track

The last desire of both was the same
To make a last passionate love, lasting forever
To repeat time and again what needed no telling
'I love you; Dear, I love you; Will love ever'

No recriminations, no 'You led us to this end'
But complete faith and surrender, lead on
Even if you are wrong, keep on going
Blind faith but more reasonable than reason

In the dark of night a flicker of light
So far away we would have missed the land
Had we passed by in the daytime
Before midnight we were on our dear island!

That was the last we were alone together
Prompt in the morning came our host
Thinking he had given us enough of privacy
Straight we plunged into the hectic beach life

First night we were led to a whirlwind tour of
The bonfires scattered through the crescent shore
On the beats of pulsating drums we danced
From bonfire to bonfire all night together

Then it's high society, the Governor threw a party
Our friend got us invited to meet high and mighty
All the paparazzi and glitterati of town were there
Bright lights, charming smiles, all polite talk

From solitude of sea we soared to social soirée
Dear! All is heavenly with you, desert or oasis
Yet these lights are slave to flicker of a switch
Smile is charming, talk polite, till turn of the back
Host is not the Governor but the government
It's not a man who invites, but Office, Company
Who is the guest? Not an individual, a friend
But a designation, a counterpart, an ex-officio
How false is the beaming smile when they meet
Presidents or Emissaries who may be plotting wars
Tomorrow, the same smile, the same kind words
Are showered on them who are sworn enemies
It's fraud, it's barter, all this host-guest business
Calling prostitution marriage or marriage becoming it
She does it for money, he for pleasure, fake love
For both anybody else would be equally welcome
The host makes an inflated expense account
Claims more than what he spent on his guests
He may submit a list of guests and what they said
As if it were a pay-off to some informer!

It's the same with other polite family invitations
They too keep count, 'We've invited so many times
They came with children and ate like hungry hogs
They have invited only once, and offered lousy food'

Some of them cannot enjoy with the family
Don't want to spend, don't believe in rotation

They go for contribution parties, each for himself
Like a sexual orgy each come with a partner

Our last night at the island was thankfully
A family get-together with few intimate friends
My friend and his family, some other mutual friends
We talked and dined and danced till the dawn

It was my last year, then last summer in the country
We bought an old Harley motorcycle for adventure
A shiny beauty in black with magical power
It was easy to drive it, difficult to control

And promptly that headstrong irresponsible girl
Rode it and banged against an army truck!
She broke her hand, me some heavy concussion
Whole varsity knew she had slipped in the bathroom!

We went all around the country on the motorcycle
Oh! Going miles and miles on lonely roads
And then to follow some unbeaten track
To some lonely niche for the lovebirds

We travelled through sea, river, plains and mountains
Amidst the islands, forests, mountains of virgin nature
We rode it but also took it with us on boat or train
Who knows who was the real traveller–we or it!

We passed through islands and narrow straits
Through changing scenery and sea
From river to green forests to ice-covered lands
Somewhere in between dreams and reality

First the seductress nymphet beacons and glides to me
Through hills and dales, meadows and groves and forests
In dripping diamond droplets dancing down cascades
Elusive embrace, glancing kiss, gone!

Sunny winter days found us basking under the sky
Amidst smooth shining boulders of dry river bed
Or on golden heath chasing butterfly dreams
Sitting around a bonfire in cold wintry nights

Dog days chased us to cool bowers along the river
Or to a soughing pine grove beside the road
We espied a waterfall in the rocky wilderness
Swam in the pool and loved behind the liquid veil

Rains deliberately found us off-guard on open lands
Like elves we frolicked under heavenly showers
And then made love on the rocks under the rains
Oh! Sun, snow, and showers, now gone out of my life!

In the small hours of morn, they meet ephemerally
Are lost again till another round of the globe
The sun and moon, stars and flowers, night and morn
Dreams and reality, sleep and wakefulness, sex and love

In the greyish dimness dark and light embrace
In the stillness forests, fields and villages slumber on
Then the gentle breeze begins to lift the misty sheet
And birds murmur the sweet entreaties of mothers

In the dusky dawn, you come to the temple
Wrapped in the pristine white warm shawl
Fresh as a rosebud bathed in dewdrops

Hallowed like the sun tip-toeing behind the hills
You light the lamp, the canopy and Gods lustre
Flame of red in the east, rays fanning skywards
Murmured prayers, chiming bells, chirping birds
Sandalwood incense, fragrance of flowering buds
Phoebus jerks the dark blanket from the treetops
Splashes them with handfuls of golden beams
Sun in the face in red border, crimson vermilion
Why enter the temple from where you have gone!

In reverse repeats morning story the setting sun
My heart capsizes in its own sanguine sea
Hope, forlorn hope, somehow keeps a lonely vigil
Patch of mellow light on highlands after the sunset
The bed is strewn with red and yellow stars
White-lily tapestry spread all through the Milky Way

Moon pines away all through the wintry night
The message of blinking stars you hear not
The heath is full of flowers in colours of rainbow
Myriad of shades, your smile hovering around me
Silent, prattling, gossiping or smiling and laughing
Buds flirting dandy bees or waltzing with foliage
A flower, a single one, only one from the milliards
Almost any would have another, other times me too
Pick I and put it tenderly under your blouse
Lingering embrace, flower between hearts, Oh! Eternity

These flowers are for flowerpots to decorate house
To make garlands or bouquets laced with hearts
To love, to kiss, to admire, to touch and pluck up
To spread over the honeymoon bed or just crush

Tall trees bear yet other flowers, not for plucking
Shower of blessings from heaven on loving hearts
Castles of colours in the air, abode of dryads
Flora-nymphet bestowing flying kisses on us

Each promenade was canopied by different flowers
We choose our walks matching your dress or mood!
Violet Jacarandas, not a trace of green foliage
Pink, red, white or yellow, all colours of love

The trees recognize us from afar and wave
Spreading fresh layer of flowers on our path
Shower of tender kisses, Oh! The rain of petals
We two in the flowery halo under the love-tree!

It's love story not love and sex story
Still less only sex story, mad desires of body
It's love which moves along, searches, finds
Both then continue the eternal love story

NOTES

1=According to the Sankhy school of Indian philosophy, there are two independent, mutually exclusive, irreducible yet supplementary principles of *Purus* and *Prakriti*, spirit and matter. *Purus* is characterized by pure consciousness, *Prakriti* by materiality and change. *Prakriti* is the primal cause of the universe, and is uncreated and imperishable. *Prakriti* is made of three 'Guns' or qualities which are inferred, not perceived–Satv manifests, Rajas activates, and Tamas restrains. Though distinguishable, they are not separable. In no object is only one of them present. In its primordial state *Prakriti* is not inert but is in a state of dynamic equilibrium. But when the reflection of the Purus is thrown into *Prakriti* the original equilibrium of the three attributes is disturbed and they try to dominate one another. Through the struggle of these three attributes, the world evolves out of *Prakriti* in various stages. Although *Prakriti* is one, the Purus are many and infinite in number. There are, therefore, an infinite number of reflections in the same *Prakriti*. And, since Prakriti is the same and has its own structure, the objective world it evolves for all the Puruses is the same.
2=See above
3=See above
4=On the death of her husband Satyavan, she followed the God of death and ultimately got back the life of her husband.
5=God of death.

Parting

Good times last not forever, not even for long
Smile fades away, love separated, life snapped
Rosebud blossoms in the dawn, drops down by dusk
All good things end, they end too, too soon

'Ere snow inflamed passions again, rains returned
I could surprise you once more with a B'day gift
We celebrate Xmas, New Year again, talk of past year
Too soon my research in your country came to an end

The Project was duly completed, thank you all!
We wept all night in tight embrace
Each time we made love we wept both
Knowing full well all this would end soon

They do anything to come to their dreamland
Fake visa and passport, identity and marriage
Once entered, declare refugee, tell stories
All is fair to get into another country!

Then doctors and engineers become taxi drivers
Or wash dishes in restaurants, be night guards
Earn lots of money, still live in mental ghettos
Really belong nowhere, be like *Trishanku*[1]

If I stayed, I would have to start all over
Perhaps to do odd jobs, meaner jobs
Perhaps my love is thought means of staying back
Or, in the struggle of life, it flies away

Better to be somebody in one's own country
Than to be nobody in comfortable alien land

But in the heat and dust and noise and crowd
You would have withered and faded away

Yet for you I was ready to do all
What is love if you do not wager all
All my misgivings I kept to my heart
But she divined them, as I did hers

She freed me saying live your life
Come back when doubts are no more
I'll always be there my love!
Then stay with me, or take me away

We made video films of our life together
Taped each other's voice and favourite songs
And made albums of our photos, forget-me-nots
I never saw them again, my eyes swelled and singed

We wrote letters to each other writing alternate words
Signed in blood and swore we're of each other forever
It took her days to take her things back home
She wept each time, how bitterly wept she!

Insane desire, persistent demand, who had asked nothing
'Give me a baby, give me your child!
Make me mother of your baby, it'll be our child
Leave some part of yourself for me to hold on to

I'll go away and live a solitary life
And will see you in the face of our child
I will seal my lips, my fate, my life
I beg you, Dear! Grant me this parting gift'

How much I wanted to beg what she was asking
But I will not make her life hostage to love
We fought, wept, she even tried to trick me
I fulfilled not even this small desire of her!

We went to aborigine province in the deep north
She took me where no foreigner had ever set foot
They came running and shouting, drums and spears
Spoke strange language but took us as sacred guests

In the evening we danced around the bonfire
Primitive dances on primitive music of drums
Welcoming, entreating us to stay, not go away
Two long-lost wandering spirits come back home

We danced our last dance together on snow!
Till mothers took away the drowsy children
The fires burnt out, food and drinks consumed
Bodies tired and sought each other to lean to

Those drums still haunt me, hammer on my head
'Stay, stay, stay, go not, go not, go not'
My heart benumbs, a feeble beat bewails in crescendo
'Go, go, go back, there is no life without her'

It was midnight but the sun was still shining
And then the sky dazzled us by the northern lights
Play of multi-colour lights and fires in the sky
As if gods were showering their benediction on us

We snuggled in each other's arms in our igloo
Loved each other in the quietest quiet around

Didn't sleep a wink all night, as if by saving
Time on sleep we will overcome fleeting time!

We came back and then life became hectic
Ah! What life, it was a funeral procession
Packing, attending a few farewell parties
Though most of them I politely declined

We had made plans for future, dependant on me
Still she knew we would never meet again
How she wept when she returned the house key
And me when she gave me her tartan skirt!

How was our last night together, did we weep
Oh! We wept till tears dried in our hearts
How does one embrace when one knows
This, this is the last time love is in arms
How long, how many times, does one kiss
When one knows that each kiss is the last
We kissed so hard, we sucked out life
Now I live yours, you live mine!
From head to toe, toe to head
All over the body again and again
As if by kissing alone I could keep you
My whole body still burns kissed by you

How does one make love for the last time
A swift love is selfish, lingering, torture
How to fake pleasure when only pain is there
We made love in tears and sobs and cries

What has she done to deserve this fathomless sorrow
Is the punishment of loving a stranger this cruel

She gave me all, more than any girl ever gave
And me, I'm going away leaving her dead

What did I give her except sadness and sorrow
I tortured her with my ego and quirks of fancy
Even my love for her I hid from the world
A proud girl, she submitted to all for love

She was stronger of us, she is still
Amidst tears and cries never said 'Don't go'
But now she is going from room to room
Wailing and sobbing and saying repeated byes

The nearer separation came she clung to me more
In her sorrow, I forgot my own gnawing pain
If both fall prey to sorrow, lost count of things
We may do something desperate, utterly foolish

I carried her in my arms, drove back last time
As I had carried her that night of last fight
I kissed her adieu, she came out of the trance
And whispered on my lips 'I'll come to airport'

At the airport were friends and well-wishers
And sure there was she, a perfect colleague
All smiles with just enough of sadness
At the parting of a peer, friend and boss

She said formally, 'Goodbye; We'll miss you'
But managed to whisper in my ear 'I love you'
I kissed her on the cheeks, our last kiss
Oh! The sweetest, the bitterest of them all!

I went to tarmac she was alone away from others
Waving good-bye but saying, 'Don't go; Come back'
I knew at that instant I was leaving my life behind
I'll come back dead to reclaim my love again

Krishn goes to meet *Radha*[2] in the woods of *Gokul*[3]
Finds her in the bower in the mango grove
All in tears and soaked in rain
A rosebud quivering under stifled sighs
'Ere she knew it he had said Good-Bye
Now she beholds him going away, away, away
Through tears, through foliage, through woods
Far away through mist and rains, going away
Krishn stops before turning the last winding path
And going away from her life forever
Glances back at her through rains and mist
Through woods, foliage and tears, from far, far away

Sliced sheet of stream dispersed by a slab of stone
Behind which on the emerald mossy mattress
Lonely nubile pink flower on a svelte stalk
Trembling in shower of tears waves Good-Bye, Bye

Stop, go not, return, not turn away
Leave me not, me leave not, not leave me
Come back, it's not too late, still come back
Come back to your love, your life, your wife!

Who will look after me when you're gone
Who will caress my mad fancies, wild desires
Who will put me to sleep with tender kisses
Oh! Who will fulfil my life in thousands of ways

Who will quarrel with you on flimsy grand issues
Who will divine the innermost thoughts of the heart
When you fall sick, God forbid, and are lonely
Who will lie beside you and soak away all the heat

But she didn't stop me, didn't block my way
Didn't pull me back to hold in tight embrace
Didn't shout, 'Stop! Don't go away, dear!
Breaking, shattering, mine heart and life'

Where am I going? To bigger things in life
I'll fight for Dharm[4] and friendship
To kingdoms and Geeta[5] and Mahabharat[6]
Love is for mere mortals, let me be God!

I turn again at the top of the stairway
She's still waving 'Goodbye, goodbye, bye'
I cross over, I lose both my love and life
The plane moves and comes back again to take off

The engines whirl, Oh! The storms in my gasps
The engine runs wildly, as runs amuck my heart
Fleetingly I see her through tears and haze
Smooth lift and senseless I fly away upwards

Oh! I came a stranger, became the Dearest
Alas! I leave now, life, miserable life!
O! Heart, Never, never, love a foreigner
I murmur, 'God bless you, Good-bye, Dearest!'

NOTES

1=He wanted to go to heaven in his mortal body. He was sent upwards by the spiritual powers of a great sage. But the gods pushed him down from above. He remained in the middle.
2=Beloved of Krishn.
3=The place where Krishn and Radha grew up.
4=Prescribed duty, religion.
5=Hindu religious and philosophical book. Krishn told it to Arjun (hero of Mahabharat, one of the five Pandav brothers) at the start of the Mahabharat war when seeing his own relatives, friends, and teacher on the opposite side, Arjun said that winning the war after killing one's beloved was not worth fighting.
6=The great war between cousin brothers Pandavs and Kauravs. Krishn helped Pandavs by becoming the charioteer of Arjun.

Uniting

That was the last she ever existed on earth
She dissolved, vanished as do vapours and mist
A rainbow is in the sky till the drop of rain
Where do beautiful things go when they disappear?

My letters came back as returns the echo
Cry of distressed heart from choked gullet
They say she left the university the next day
And moved with the family to native province

Why she went, didn't even wait for my letters
My promises, my plans, calling her or my return
She knew all was in vain if I could not
Take her or stay back when we were together

She loved me as none ever loved none
But she was proud too, she would not
Wait for me to come back to take her
Or follow me alone on my bidding

I left her where each place is pregnant with memories
She has run away from those places, remembrances
My name will never come on her lips, but
Each moment she will still live by me

I moulded her body, her thoughts, her life
How could she now change without breaking
She'll miss morning kisses, presence around
Surprise divining of desires, love quarrels

She would moan all night for her lost love
And lie awake for my embrace, my caress

In dark nights, all alone, she would
Whisper my name and cry and lie awake

Often I think she was not mortal but
A spirit of Nature in borrowed body
Who fell for a mortal against her Will
Is now punished by banishment for the Sin

She was a spirit, she could give her so wantonly
And forsake the family, the world for me
So dear was I to her, yet she could leave me
On the spur of the moment and regret not, never

Her heart was the canyon rock which let
The tender stream of my love cut to the quick
It embraces ever so softly, then lets it slip by
Bestowing some lingering mossy farewell kisses

She still haunts those places where we loved
And wails and wails for her tender love lost
Nature goddess lets her not return to her kingdom
Amidst humans she wanders bemoaning her mortal love

If I return there I would find the spirit
And will give back her the body
As one who has heard a melodious song
Can hum the words when music alone is played

Man aspires for the body, woman for the heart
She gives her heart first, he kisses the lips
She wagers all, man saves for the second round
She leaves behind all, gives all, he grabs

Dear! Nobody sides with you, nor man nor woman
Father calls me a fool, mother thinks I suffered
Calls names, why are you after my innocent child
Brothers call me Lover Boy, sisters search for a bride!

Surprise! More than men women condemn you
Sisters say, 'They know magic, you're bewitched
The most eligible bachelor, all the world to choose
You chose a girl who has already disappeared'!

Friends say, 'Love is a passing fancy, an infatuation'
But then almost all things in life are so!
We are infatuated with parents, brothers, sisters
In time we forget them and fight for property

For a few years we are puritan, idealist and moralist
This or that ism means more than life to us
Then a time comes, all our illusions are shattered
And we live life selfishly just for ourselves

But nobody calls them passing fancies, infatuations
Love of Eve is often condemned as such
They say, 'Be faithful to a friend'
Who would hang till death a Lady Killer?

'Love is another thing, marriage something else
You loved, you enjoyed her, now forget her
If you marry her, love would die, you'll hate her
Marry another, your first love will ever be there!'

They too lose all, foolishly or wantonly
In anger, in sloth, in senseless wars

Condemn not them the world, sometimes applauds
Why then when it's love, they call it stupidity

Unreal, dark, and death to real, light, and immortality
Lead me, O! God, prayed our ancestors
We know not what's reality, light and immortality
And hate unreality, darkness and death foolishly
Is light what dazzles night in the city
Truth life of chasing illusions of fame and fortune
Immortality to be known by some mortals for some time
Then better give me unreality, darkness, and death

Since birth, we are fixated upon and run
To the lighted towns from dark villages
To ever wanting luxuries from simple necessities
And to anonymity of knowing multitude from solitude
So when she offered me love in a faraway land
I searched for fame and fortune
I hesitated a moment too long
And lost all–you!

In the vast expanse of multi-dimensional multiverse[1]
How infinitesimal and ephemeral is human existence
How trivial, how meaningless are human aspirations
What we think is caught is already slipping away!

Satan plays strange tricks to make man suffer
He said, 'You could have both, here and hereafter
Fame and Fortune and still retain your Love'
He tricked me and now I've lost both

How could Satan trick me when after loving you
I had no desires, no dreams, no aspirations

For glittering gold and thundering applause of masses
You fulfilled my life so completely, so overwhelmingly

Dear! I'm duped so badly, I can't even protest
I came to shining lights, now they blind me
The more sumptuous feast is laid before me
The more I miss you to offer the first bite

Bathed in limelight amidst shower of applause
How much I miss a slender silhouette by my side!
When happiness tries to embrace, fondle and kiss me
The sorrow within me goes numb, ravished

But for me now the time has come
When a man has to resolve and assert
What he wants from life, in death
I desire nothing except your love

Now you are part of my Self
Nay, a new whole is made of our Selves
Without you, I live another man's life
At best a crippled life, partial life
Three lives in one, O! God spare
One eats and drinks and laughs and weeps
The other goes along till one day
It knows they are two, they are different
The Third is beyond both, comprises both
It's not me, We, Unity-in-Duality
The flame leaps out of fire
Returns to it, lost in it!

I'm We, yet much of both is left behind
My Me understands not Our We

Our We cares not for me or you or the world
For our We let Me cease to be
My We is incomplete without you
Why should I live life of another in my Me?
Three lives in One torment
How much, how long could the soul suffer?

They say mind and matter are different
Then how one affects the other?
They beat me, your image is unshattered
My body betrays not, I'm with you

If mind is matter, how could there be
Vivid imagination, foresight, future planning
Can the atoms be arranged
In an imaginary future configuration!

How could there be cause and effect
Between things separated by time and space
How could Zeno's arrow fly
Achilles overtake tortoise, time elapse
Arrow is where it is or not, moves it not
For every overtaking tortoise moves further
For every portion of time to elapse
Its half, its half, ad infinitum must elapse

For me nothing else is meaningful, all seems illusion
Only reality is the time and place we were together
I step out and find ourselves on the beach
Till street urchins follow me shouting 'loony, loony'

Why condemn me if my mind
Gives not false dimensions and concepts

But projects a world of love, cloaks all in love
The whole of reality for me is love

The Élan Vital, the Will, the Idea
The Intellect, Intuition, Consciousness
Form and Matter, the Four Causes
All is Love, Love is All

Fools, they cut a slice of illusion
From the ever-changing flux of reality
Like the multitude of snapshots of cinematography
Wonder about motion and emotion, time and space

I grasp Love, the Whole of the flux
And see all in love and love in all
My world is one dimensional, a Unity
My Absolute is Love, my Love Absolute

For me love is Sat, Chit, and Anand[2]
What could be greater, truer, more beautiful
Than the reality, consciousness and bliss
Of love, of my love, of our love

How could two and two make four
Both, in Math and in nature
Science predict nature, nature follow science
Unless all this is a great hoax played by mind
Like a magician who puts rabbits in the hat
And then pulls them out as if newly discovered
How could anything new be known by reason
How could mind jump from unknown to known
An electron, a tiny particle, moving in its orbit
The greatest scientist is not certain, can't tell

Both its position and momentum at a time
He can talk only in probabilities, in statistics
An electron is only in a probable energy level
Its energy, its orbit, probability, not certainty
What of parallel worlds, the dubiety of life
God threw the dice, we count the pips
Peering hard inside an atom, the proud physicist
Espies suddenly a particle where there was none
Finds virtual, twin, and mirror-image particles
Reacting across their universe without rhyme and reason

If matter is illusion, mind a hoax
What remains except the Spirit
Some feelings, some instincts, some intuitions
And over-powering all, the Love
All is then spaceless-timeless, infinite possibilities
We impose space-time and reduce to potential finites
Laws of science reduced to strict probabilities
Life and universe just become a wave function

Out of the infinite snapshots of life
We select a few, a very limited few
Moving them in a movie projector
See life in time and space, cause and effect!

Out of randomly flying cards
We select a few and arrange them
According to four suits and numbers
How compact is our this pack of cards!

We prisoners of space-time, cause-effect
See life in self-perpetuating continuity birth to death
Like wandering mind why cannot our body be free

To choose at will a different probable set of life
So that while sitting in a room we do not continue to be
But the next instant, nay the same instant, be outside it
From thereon lead a quite different life
As with a flick of remote we change TV channel

They have gagged me, chained to the bed
They scorch, pierce and give vile things to drink
They stand around me and devise new tortures
Dear! I have come to hell from our paradise

When it's sunny outside, flowers all around
It snows in drifting flakes, rains in torrents
You call me out, we talk, frolic and make love
They know not how I went out, when I came in

Sometimes you come up, striding the window
Or walk right through the closed doors
We talk and talk and laugh and laugh
Then we make love and you depart in the morn

Later you stayed even when they came
Sometimes you moved things, they were amazed
Blinds! They never saw you, said that
My agitated mental state caused psychokinesis!

They try to explain by some such names
When I'm hot in the sun, drenched in the rain
Your fragrance lingering on me, a rose on the bed
Or when I tell them what happened outside the walls

I wandered with you all over the Island of Circe
Your love I thought a spell, returned sans you

Dear! Too late realize I, you are my Penelope
This, this my home, is but the Continent of Circe

Sadists! You numb me, now she has come
She is snatching at the chains, howling like storms
She is tossing and tumbling me, calling me
Pierce my whole body, I'll go to her

The drums, the drums, they are beating wildly
I'm free, I'm bound to her, we float in the air
Were we ever parted? We are two-in-one
Eternity to eternity, we are two Entangled[3] Souls!

NOTES

1=According to latest Theory of Everything and M-Theory which attempt to explain everything by one unified field theory, there are multi-dimensions (11, possibly 26) and infinite co-existing parallel universes.
2=*Sat,* Being, the existence which is common to all things; *Chit,* Consciousness (of existence); *Anand,* Pure Joy or Bliss.
3=In Quantum Mechanics, Entangled Particles are pair of particles which are in such a mysterious bond that altering the state (for example, polarization) of one of the pair, instantaneously (i.e. with a speed greater than that of light, which, according to Theory of Relativity, is not possible) alters the state of the other particle. Einstein called it, 'spooky action at a distance'.